... left against new laws against demonstrations is attacked by the right. In the melee a demonstrator is coshed. He dies later in hospital. His name is Nicky.

Who killed Nicky? His best friend Albie is determined to find out. He discovers a baffling world of police corruption, trendy liberal lawyers, far right extremists and political violence. Albie has never been political but everyone assumes he must be? Is he?

Roger Mills

Bad Fun

COLLINS

LIONS · TRACKS

First published in Great Britain in 1989 in Lions Tracks

Lions Tracks is an imprint of
the Children's Division, part of
the Collins Publishing Group,
8 Grafton Street, London W1X 3LA

Printed in Great Britain
by William Collins Sons & Co. Ltd, Glasgow

When all the fuss had died down, the times that Albie remembered the best were those summer afternoons in Nicky's room during the last term. Exams were crap. They'd never pass them anyway, so they never went to school. Albie brought his records round.

Nicky's room had a single bed, a thin cord carpet and a cheap record deck. He kept terrapins in a tank and his grandad's WW1 medals in a jar. The walls were given over entirely to the local league team – United. Nicky would get his dart board out and they'd spend a couple of hours chucking darts. The board was suspended on the door by a rusty dart driven deep. Albie always won, so Nicky would get bored and pin up a picture of the Duchess of York clambering into a helicopter and see how near he could get an arrow to her bum. Then he would make coffee.

They'd get Nicky's old Judge Dredd comics out and read them quietly for a while and then turn the radio on and jump around doing Prince impersonations when his records came on. Nicky would get angry at the DJ and swear at the radio whenever he made a stupid DJ joke. They'd get excited just mucking about, really. They were the only movement in a still world. Desert rats. With the window to the backyard wide open, and the warm breeze drifting in, they felt as if a million years lay before them. There was an anticipation of future glory. Days were long. Something was bound to happen sooner or later in one of those shining endless hours.

Nicky's mum and dad worked all day and didn't know

about his pellet-gun. *Wasn't like a real gun*, Nicky explained, *but it could take an eye out or worse if you stuck it up someone's nose.* He had got it off a Turk down Brick Lane early one market day. That was where he got the tin helmet from as well.

Nicky and Albie took it in turns to hold the old ARP hat in front of their faces while the other fired pellets at it. Every time the gun cracked Albie couldn't help but blink no matter which side of the tin mask he was on. When he was crouched on the bed holding the helmet before him, he'd jerk his head back as well. It was exciting to imagine the pellet just fractions away from the tip of his nose, coming at him like spit one minute and then stopped dead the next.

On one of those late afternoons, as Albie was looking out of the back window, he saw a robin hopping along the back wall. As he watched it spring along the red bricks, he lined it up in the sights of the pellet-gun. He toyed with the idea of squeezing the trigger, hardly realising that he meant it. The bird had seemed so far away. It dropped like a chunk of loose masonry. Albie and Nicky said they wished they hadn't done it, like the blame was equal. But they didn't dwell on it much because Nicky's mum and dad had come home. Nicky tucked the gun away between the comics and football socks on the top shelf of his wardrobe. They said goodbye. That night Albie cried in his bed for the robin and wondered if Nicky was doing the same.

You are listening to LBC Radio News...

...The controversial march through the West End of London, planned for tomorrow, November 5th, is to go ahead. This follows a pledge by several right-wing organisations not to mount a counter-demonstration as initially threatened. Their withdrawal is as sudden as it is unexpected...

...The march, organised by a range of left-wing groups, voluntary organisations and trade unions to protest about the new laws on the right to hold demonstrations, has been causing consternation in the capital because of the risk of a violent clash...

...The Commissioner of the Metropolitan Police, who had considered banning the march even though the new laws have not yet been passed by Parliament, expressed relief. He says he is now confident there will be no trouble...

Chapter 1

Barefoot, Albie stood at the tower-block window, jingling the chunky quids in his pocket. From up here you could see all the way to nowhere, and now that it was evening tiny lights stretched all the way there.

It was starting to rain again and if he got his feet wet it would be all his own fault. He could have spent the five coins which rattled round his pocket on getting his shoes resoled, but he'd chosen to save them for tonight, Saturday night. He pulled the coins out for inspection. Queued up on a single finger, piled up on a thumb or flat in the palm of his hand, they still didn't add up to much.

After Albie and Nicky had separated earlier in the day, Albie had spent the afternoon looking round the shops in Oxford Street. He couldn't afford to buy anything, so he had slowly made his way back to the East End on foot. Mum had left a note to say she was out shopping. There was nothing on the telly so he'd spent some time in his room with the day before's newspaper. The girl in the picture wore a tight leather mini-skirt with a chunky zip right up the back. He imagined himself unzipping it, slowly.

A thunderstorm had come on suddenly to dampen the end of what had been a cold yet bright day. Lying across the bed, he heard Mum, just returned, talking to the vests, shirts and pants as she gathered them in from the small tenth-floor balcony. ''...And you were nearly dry too.''

It was then he'd got up to study the dark horizon and plot the night ahead. To save money, he usually walked half the way to the Three Johns pub before catching the bus. That way he cut his fare in half. On an evening like this, however, with a hole in his shoe, it would mean standing at the bar with a soggy foot all night. Still, if he'd had the shoes repaired he couldn't have afforded to go out anyway.

As always on a Saturday, Ablie planned to arrive at the Three Johns just before ten. Rummy, Dirk, Nicky and Tommy with the one eye would all have been there an hour, would have downed three pints each and be in the middle of a fourth. He'd go straight to the bar before searching them out. He knew damned well they'd be up by the television set as usual, but with a half in his hand as he approached they'd be no question of him having to buy drinks. After they'd knocked back theirs, however, he'd be included in the round of whoever was laying out next, and the next, and all the nexts after that. He'd be on pints then, of course. All the lads knew Albie's tactics and Albie knew they knew but then everyone knew Albie was on the dole.

Albie watched the rain.

"We'll have to cut out those chocolate biscuits you like, Albie," said Mum as she joined Albie in the kitchen, "they're just too expensive." She was preparing the evening meal and clipping on a plastic flower earring at the same time.

"That's OK," replied Albie. His nose was pressed up against the window. He could see flames and surprises of light. He heard bangs.

"And I reckon we can make a nice stew for Mondays out of the chicken we don't finish on Sundays. That'll be all right, won't it?"

"That'll be fine."

"Economy's the order of the day now, you know?" She donned an apron to protect her dress. "You don't have to give up much when you economise, you just have to be more sensible." Albie was trying to concentrate on the hole-in-shoe problem, looking to see if it was still raining. It was. He saw something else too, a man in a furry coat moving out of the rain to the shelter of the block opposite.

Mum continued: "You wouldn't believe what Mrs Jay told me in the supermarket today, Albie. She said that when her and Harry, that's her husband, took Desperate, that's their dog, for a run on Hackney Marshes, he slipped off the lead and ran into the bushes. And when they found him he was whining like a puppy and had great chunks taken out of him. Big teeth marks all over." Mum hacked open a tin of chopped tomatoes as she spoke and kicked off her fluffy slippers into the broom cupboard. Pulling on her shoes she poured the tomatoes into the pan with the fried onions. "And then when I got back home I heard on the radio that there's a bear loose on Hackney Marshes."

Albie turned away from the window and made the expression that people make when someone tells them there's a bear loose on Hackney Marshes.

"Well, rumour of it, anyway," Mum said.

Albie watched his mum doing everything at once. She was painting her face now, artist and model all at the same time. He felt he'd like to offer to do things to help her and felt bad that she didn't think she could ask him to heat the mince or prepare the salad. But he knew full well that if she ever did ask him then he'd have to refuse. Just because he didn't work didn't mean that he could hang around doing odd jobs all day. It was a stupid attitude, he knew. Everything was sizzling nicely and Mum started to cut five fingers of carrot into little chunks. She took time to tug a grey hair from her blonde thatch and renew the red round her mouth.

Albie sometimes pictured the flat as a doll's house with the top off, an aerial view revealing the daily doings within the tiny boxes which were the rooms. Here's Mum, jumping out of bed, tidying round, giving the bog a good old scrub out, washing Albie's shirts. Here's Albie, kipping. And here's Mum, slitting open the mail with all the red writing over it and checking what's left in her bank account. Here's Albie rubbing his eyes a bit and he wants to pee and Mum brings him a cuppa but he's turning over. There's toast going on and it's Mum who's making it. There's Albie getting up and he's washing and stumbling all over the place and it's Mum's fault that the toast's cold. Here's Mum going out of the door. She's a machinist. Albie scans the press for work. Sweet FA. More kipping. Mum's back. Evening already. Albie can smell grub. Mum's making it, Albie's waiting for it. Here's both of them eating it in front of the telly. They're not talking much because Mum's got nothing to talk about except work and Albie can't even do that. And then Mum does the washing up and Albie feels sick of it all. Here he is, late at night. In his room he swears aloud at the city far below because a strong enough obscenity blots out the thought that this is what forever is.

"Well, you never know," continued Mum. "It might have escaped from a zoo or something. Stranger things have happened." Then she dropped the tea tray she had forgotten was under her arm. The clatter brought Albie out of his depression. He breathed hard on the window. It made a little shape, a bit like a cloud. Mum pushed the stiff column of spaghetti into boiling water. The skinny stork legs went all weak at the knees when they hit the water. She checked the bubbly sauce. Albie could still see the man in the furry coat below. His head appeared out of the block's entrance hall every few minutes. Mum took two plates from the sideboard and put them on the shiny white surface by the oven. She untied the apron and put her coat on.

"Hey, Mum, do you see that bloke down there? Standing just out of the rain. I saw him hanging about the other night. See him? He's got a briefcase."

"I'll look in a second, Albie," she said. "I'm late enough for the evening class as it is. The girls won't thank me for keeping them waiting outside on a night like this."

Mum divided the spaghetti and salad out on to the plates and picked up the opera glasses she kept by the window. She'd told Albie that she'd not meant to steal them. She'd absentmindedly put them into her bag after a Palladium matinée and was too embarrassed to take them back.

"Can't see a thing," she said and started to eat her food standing up.

Albie held the glasses up to his eyes. There was no one there.

Albie tried to tuck some cardboard from a Weetabix packet into his shoe to cover the hole, but found that it squashed his little toe. Oh well, it looked as if the rain was easing up anyway.

The rain had stopped completely by the time Albie left the building. Tiny explosions of green, red and yellow still punctured the black sky and Albie realised that it must be Guy Fawkes night. Kids had been touting for money with their guys for what seemed like months, not that this year's range of guys had been up to much. No kids in the streets now, though. They'd all be at the parks watching the big firework displays. Not many people in the East End had their own yards to light fireworks in.

On busy Whitechapel High Street Albie waited so long for a bus that he found himself walking from stop to stop and by the time the big red double-decker passed, mocking him with exhaust raspberries, he decided he might as well do the whole distance on foot. It meant he could watch the fireworks. Albie remembered his own childhood bonfire nights, how Dad wouldn't let him light the blue touchpaper and how he couldn't wait for the time when he could – just to show Dad. But by the time he was big enough, Dad had snuffed it.

Albie quickened his pace. He relished these Saturday nights in the pub. Albie had known the lads since primary school – well-built Rummy, chubby Dirk, and Tommy with the one eye who towered above them all. But Nicky was his best friend of all. With a pint in his hand and the lads all round, shoulder to shoulder in a boozy scrum, it seemed to Albie that nothing was a problem anymore.

The pub came into sight with its silly, frilly awnings and fake carriage lamps that shone like a row of small lighthouses in the smoky bonfire night. The Three Johns was noisy tonight, noisier than usual, and it was usually too noisy. Albie could see his friends bunched up beneath the television set just as he'd expected. The highlights of an earlier football match were being shown on the screen. There was no Nicky, but perhaps he was in the toilet. Albie slapped one of his precious pound coins down on the bar, purchased a half, and joined the lads.

Rummy was attacking with no one defending: "...and I tell you, they're all communists, these people who go round protesting about everything. If they don't like it here why don't they bugger off to Russia? That's what I say."

"What's up with him?" Albie asked Dirk.

"The news on the telly just now started him off," Dirk replied. "There was a protest march today which ended up in a punch-up with the police in the West End, a place called Circle Square." Dirk saw that Albie had already drained his glass and took him off to the bar to set him up a pint, leaving Tommy with the one eye the sole beneficiary of Rummy's lecture. Tommy with the one eye

13

winked conspiratorially at Albie above Rummy's short-cropped head just to show he wasn't taking it too seriously.

"Seen anything of Nicky this evening?" asked Dirk as they elbowed their way to the sparkle-mirrored bar. "I'm surprised he hasn't shown up yet."

"I'm sure we'll see his face before long," said Albie.

The Three Johns was decorated in what Albie supposed was a sort of upper-class brothel style, very popular in the East End. Lights were low and fluffy carpets met furry seats which must have been hell to scrape the puke off. Usually the sounds were disco, but the telly took over whenever Arsenal were on. The landlord had once had a brother in the reserves.

Dirk was waiting to be served and was saying something about a birthday. But Albie wasn't listening. "*Big* trouble, was it?" he shouted over the noise of the TV, "you said something about a punch-up at a demonstration." He loosened his collar in the heat.

"I got no sympathy, me," said Dirk, fanning his face with the crisp tenner he was trying to lure the barmaid with. "Some silly sod got damaged. And that was after the right-wingers cancelled their counter-march so as to avoid a punch-up. Shows who the troublemakers are, don't it? You still on lager?"

Yes, lager, and Albie knocked it back quickly. Nicky didn't show and Nicky still didn't show even after another couple of pints. Rummy and Tommy with the one eye finally joined them at the bar. Drinks on Rummy; it was his birthday. He asked after Nicky as well. All the time Albie watched the door. Groups of blokes came in looking for groups of girls looking for groups of blokes. But Nicky didn't come in at all. The circle was incomplete. Albie's hopes of a pleasant boozy evening sank with every gulp of lager he took. He knew that time was getting on because

14

the televised football match was well into its second half. It was a dirty game with players going down like Guinness at a wake.

Rummy mentioned that he'd seen Albie and Nicky getting on a bus that morning and asked where they had been off to. Albie supped deep into his pint before answering, his eyes glancing over to the television screen. "We went to United's grounds," he said finally. "We didn't want to go far, see?"

"Who were they playing?" asked Tommy with the one eye.

"Er, Southampton."

"Oh yeah," said Rummy. "Good game, was it?"

"No. Boring. Nil-nil draw."

"That can't be right," said Dirk. "I heard on the results that United had stuck one in from a penalty kick."

"Oh yeah, they did. But that was the only goal. It was a One-Nil draw. Well, what I mean really is that we were so bored that we left before the goal." Albie breathed hard. He'd never known it so hot in the pub before.

Tommy with the one eye was looking worried. "But I heard on the radio that there were two goals scored in the first eleven minutes."

Albie sponged his brow with his sleeve. "Yes," he said, "but me and Nicky get bored easily."

"You feeling all right, Albie? You look a bit pale," said Dirk.

"Well, I'm not surprised you two got bored if you went down United's grounds," said Rummy. "It must have been lonely standing on the terraces all by yourselves."

"What're you on about?" asked Albie.

Rummy smiled politely. "United played away today. They went to Southampton's ground. So where *did* you go then, you and Nicky?"

All the lads turned to Albie for some sort of explanation.

At that moment, a commotion started amongst those who had been watching the football. A pained cry let rip from the depths of a dozen beery guts, for on the telly screen a NEWSFLASH sign had replaced the slow motion replay of a particularly tasty dribble from mid-field which had resulted in a winning goal. Rummy was fanning Albie with his jacket but he had one eye on the screen. "If this is more bloody news about that bleedin' demonstration march I'll..."

A serious-faced newsreader appeared on the screen. A youth dead in Circle Square. The boy reported earlier taken to hospital had since died. They flashed a picture of Nicky up on the screen.

Chapter 2

It was bright and cold and Nicky and Albie were walking.
They were walking through a park, more as a sort of short
cut than a visit. Nicky said that he didn't care for parks
himself. He didn't like the country either. Grass and trees
belonged to ruddy-faced farmers who waved sticks at you
whenever you went near them, which wasn't very nice.
And parks were a bit like the countryside. He then talked
about the chips he was eating. He wondered if they tasted
of anything at all, or if he just liked them because they were
all hot and squidgy. Albie said that there were lots of posh
houses over on the other side of the park, white and
elegant. Albie reckoned they were owned by airline pilots
or something who were no doubt at this very moment
between crisp white sheets with crisp white air hostesses.
Nicky thought it was more likely yuppies. He put
everything down to yuppies. As they got closer they saw
that the buildings were a lot tattier than they'd thought.
In fact they were downright wrecks and when they got
closer still they could see they didn't have any roofs. Nicky
and Albie threw some chips in the duck pond for a bit and
Nicky said that the kid beside them was talking to himself.
He wasn't though, it was a transistor radio. Nicky said that
once it was only Joan of Arc who heard voices, now they
were everywhere, floating on the airwaves. Albie said that
nothing was what it seemed any more. The park keeper
said not to throw chips at the ducks and that they should
leave. Albie said that he was fed up with rambling anyway,
and Nicky said that he'd warned him the country was
always like that.

Albie opened his eyes. A man he had never seen before was sitting at the foot of his bed. He was big and broad-shouldered beneath his coat and a toupee sat uneasily on his bollard-shaped head. When he saw Albie's eyes open, he smiled. It was a big wide smile that elevated his ears. Albie closed his eyes again and hoped that the apparition would be gone when he looked again. It was.

Albie felt fine while he was lying down. It was when he sat up and leaned against the headboard that he felt things shift in his head. Perhaps if he sat still. Perhaps if he sat *very* still...

It was cold in the bedroom and he pulled the sheets up to cover his bare chest and shoulders. The only problem then was that his feet were uncovered by the manoeuvre.

Christ! What on earth had he done to himself?

Oh yes, he'd been out boozing the night before with Rummy, Dirk and Tommy with the one eye. That was it, it was Rummy's birthday. Drinks all round, quite a few rounds, in fact. Just another hangover.

Albie eased himself out of bed, sat on the edge with his feet on the carpet and scientifically cranked his body up and forward until he was standing upright in the way he'd seen human beings stand. He pulled on his jeans. In the bathroom he opened and shut his mouth at the mirror, a less than attractive sight for his sore, red eyes. He ran the taps for a few seconds and then plunged his hands in deep to begin the cleaning procedure. The scalding water helped wash some of the hangover away but it took Alka-Seltzer and a mug of hot black coffee to remind his body that it hadn't always been like this.

Albie finished off the coffee and thought about another when he heard the rhubarb-rhubarb of conversation coming from the living room. It was early on Sunday

18

morning. Albie couldn't think who Mum might be entertaining at this hour. He turned the radio on and let it play quietly in the background. Church music. Albie hated all that organ music stuff but thought that it might be good for him. Someone started to read a sermon but Albie felt well enough now to turn it off.

Albie entered the living room to find Mum sitting on the sofa beside a man, all snug like he was a relative over for Christmas or something. He was big and broad-shouldered beneath his coat and a toupee sat uneasily on his bollard-shaped head. When he saw Albie, he smiled. It was a big wide smile that elevated his ears. It was the man he'd dreamed up in the night. It was all mixed up with another dream he'd had about Nicky being dead.

Chapter 3

Albie noticed that the man didn't use his safety belt. He fastened his own securely, though, and not just because the man was a copper. The man put his foot down on all the corners. They were well over the speed limit as they hit Whitechapel. The man took a short cut down the wrong way of a one way and pulled up sharp outside a police station.

Albie started to undo his safety belt. "Don't bother with that," said the man and jumped out of the car. They were the first words spoken since they had left the flat. When Albie had entered the living room the huge figure had leapt up and bounded towards him, hand outstretched like some rampant arm-wrestler. The man had introduced himself as Detective Inspector Cobb, and asked if Albie wanted to get his shoes on as they were going for a ride.

As she hurried Albie into his jacket, Mum told him she'd thought it best to call the police after he'd been brought home by the lads in such a terrible state the night before.

"Your Mum's right, Albie. You can help us find out exactly how this Circle Square accident happened. Believe me, we want to get to the bottom of all this, don't you worry." The man nodded mournfully and added that he only had forty-five minutes before he went off duty so they'd better make it snappy.

As he waited for Detective Inspector Cobb, Albie looked at himself in the rear-view mirror. His eyes were black and his hair was sticking out at all angles where he'd slept on it funny. He looked like – what was the expression? – death warmed up.

He wound down the side window to breathe in some of the chilly Sunday. The ache in his head had stopped short of murder but now his stomach was threatening GBH. Cobb bounced back into the driver's seat. "Sorry. Had a phone call to make. I thought we might go to a nice little riverside pub I know in Wapping. We can have a chat over a drink."

"A drink?"

"Yeah. Or would you rather talk at the station?"

They drove to the river.

The car hit nought fast outside the pub. Baskets of drooping flowers swayed in the wind above their heads as they reached the pub doors. A high time for old Wapping, said Cobb, lots of moneyed people snapping up the riverside dwellings. He made it sound good.

Above the shop next door a clock insisted on ten fifty-five. Cobb drew his car keys from the inside pocket of his overcoat and tapped one of them on the pub door. "Open up, you old bastard. It's me, Cobb, and I'm thirsty."

A voice from within: "We're not open yet. Buzz off or I'll call the law."

"Silly old sod," whispered Cobb, then bellowed, "I *am* the law," at the hunched shape beyond the glass.

Keys rattled, bolts clanked and the door was prised out of its frame. An old man stared out. "Cobb," he said and stepped back into darkness. They followed him in. A young man stood cleaning pint glasses behind the bar. Cobb ordered a couple of pints of special. The young man made a show of looking at his wristwatch but pulled the pints regardless.

They sat at one of the pub tables. Albie stared at his beer as the old man shuffled round them, muttering to himself and emptying the contents of the previous night's ashtrays

21

into a black plastic rubbish bag.

"Good pub this, Albie," said Cobb, "tourists love it. Japs and Swedes come by the coach-load to take pictures. I bring my sister and brother-in-law here in the summer. He's in the force too. A brother-in-law in more ways than one, eh?" Cobb laughed and took a swig of his beer. He offered to get Albie a plateful of something. "Sausage, beans and mash would be all right, wouldn't it?" Albie didn't get a chance to answer. Cobb rushed to the bar to place an order with the resentful young man behind it.

Cobb returned to the table and immediately started speaking. His voice took on a business-like almost robot-ic tone. "Yesterday at two forty-five Nicky Turner was admitted to Bart's Hospital with extensive head injuries. He was already unconscious. Police found his name and address on his bus pass. His mum was at the bedside when he died at just after four. When I was speaking to your mum this morning, she told me you'd been out with Nicky yesterday."

Albie moved his hand away from his pint, tucked his little finger into the corner of his mouth and tore away a slither of fingernail.

Cobb continued, "Nicky Turner was involved in a riot situation in Circle Square. I understand that you spent the day with him. I think that together we can get to the bottom of what happened."

"Is Nicky really dead?" asked Albie and Cobb said he looked like he could do with another pint.

"Tell me, Albie," said the policeman, watching him drain his second glass, "why did you go on that march?"

Somebody was calling.

Albie jerked his head around. A small man in a grubby sheepskin coat and a little leather cap was standing by the

22

pub door. "Blimey, you must be desperate," he called out. "Barely opening time."

The man came over, and, temporarily removing a hand from his baggy coat pocket, slapped Cobb on the shoulder. The man had looked quite young from a distance, but close up Albie could see that he was wrinkled and that wispy hair blew out from under the titchy cap. "Well, what are you doing here then?"

"We're trying to have a little chat," Cobb told him.

The man laughed. "He's a one, eh?" he said to Albie.

"This is Albie," said Cobb, "he had a friend die on that demonstration yesterday. They were together in Circle Square."

The small man sat down in one of the vacant chairs and pushed the cap back across his head. "Good mate, was he?" he asked.

Albie didn't feel ill any more. In fact, he felt really good. The pints must have helped. Albie opened up a little hatch in his brain marked *Nicky* and began to pull all the memories out, struggling and biting a bit. Albie told the small man and Cobb that he and Nicky had both been in the reserves of the local "Whitechapel Wanderers" amateur team. But they had first met years ago at school.

"During the holidays, me and Nicky and all my other mates – Rummy, Dirk and Tommy with the one eye – used to play the knockers game. Know what that means?" Albie laughed. "Well, we'd all bundle into a minivan that Dirk's older brother hired and bomb over to the posh boroughs. We'd be given all this really crappy stuff, things like ironing board covers that had been made too small or tea towels that dissolve when they get wet. We'd start at one end of the road with a boxful and work our way along knocking at all the doors. We'd flash people these little cards that Dirk's older brother gave us. People never looked too closely. We'd tell them we were collecting for handicapped kids. They'd usually buy something. It was only a few quid to them but it would add up. Dirk's older brother collected it all in and just gave us pocket money. We were really young kids then, see? Didn't realise we were being ripped off too. It's funny. I have to laugh. Sometimes people wouldn't buy anything and we'd think they were the scum of the earth, not giving anything to help the handicapped."

It was the little man in the leather cap's turn to buy Albie a drink. Albie couldn't imagine why he was telling them all this. There were so many memories. The drink made them topple over each other. He realised that he was rambling once more, rambling about Nicky.

Albie excused himself and went to the toilet. He had been so caught up in his thoughts that he had failed to notice that the pub was now full of people. He had to push his way through. His head swam.

"Here," shouted the young man behind the bar as Albie emerged. "Your copper pal ordered some food for you. It's been ready for ages. I called out twice."

Albie took the food back to the table. Cobb was alone.

"Your mate gone?" asked Albie.

"My mate? No mate of mine." Cobb got up. "Look, Albie, I have to be off. I think we've gone about as far as we can for the time being. I'll be in touch. Anything else you want to tell me?"

Albie put the now cold plate of sausages, beans and mash on the table, realising that he had no knife and fork. He sat down heavily, staring at the plateful and feeling waves of nausea run through him.

"Well, is there anything you want to ask *me*, then?" demanded the policeman, patting his toupee.

"Well, just...what happens next?"

Cobb shrugged. "We'll just have to wait and see," he said. "It's in the hands of a higher authority now, Albie."

24

Chapter 4

Albie found a note taped to the front door when he got back home. AT BRENDA'S. COME QUICK. At first he couldn't imagine who Brenda could be, where she might be and why on earth Mum should want him to join her there. Then he remembered that Brenda was Nicky's mum. He legged it sharpish.

It was Albie's own mum who opened the door to the Turners' house. Her eyes were red and puffy. She told him they all were in the kitchen and as he followed her in he realised that he was expecting to see Nicky there like he always did when he called. Nicky would be finishing off his tea, gobbling it down because he wanted to go off with Albie.

Nicky's mum was in the kitchen, standing upright and holding on to the cooker behind her back, clutching it like she was expecting someone to snatch it away from her. Nicky's dad was sitting in a chair. His head was deep in his hands so Albie could see a bald patch he hadn't noticed before. Nicky's dad was a hard man, had been mixed up in all sorts of petty villainy; that was why it was difficult to watch him sobbing. But he was angry too.

"Jesus wept," he cried.

Mum started to speak. "Norris didn't see Nicky at all before he died, Albie." *Norris*. Albie had always found it really funny that Nicky's dad was called Norris. But he wasn't laughing. "He was helping out on his cousin's stall in the market when a policeman took him aside. He just said that Nicky had got himself in a spot of bother and took him down the police station."

25

Norris spoke. The voice came from a million miles under the sea and the words were driven back into his mouth by waves of tears as he gulped for air. "The bastards didn't let on Nicky was dying. Just kept asking me why he would have been on that march, what sort of people he was mixed up with. And all the time Brenda was there with him by herself."

Mrs Turner was breathing deep, just holding on to the cooker like she'd keel over if she didn't. Now it was her turn. "Norris wasn't brough along until long after Nicky had died. I was holding his hand all the time but he never came round."

Albie was feeling very warm. He didn't like looking at the Turners because every time he looked at them it seemed they were looking at him and he got the idea that they had the idea that somehow it was all his fault and he didn't like that idea at all. It would have been nice to be able to say something comforting and then clear off. And then Nicky's dad said, "Rummy told me that you were on that march with Nicky. It must have been you that made him go on it. It was you that got our son killed."

Albie began to wish even more that he had an exit line. He hadn't uttered a word since entering the house and he realised that there was absolutely nothing to say. You couldn't talk back the dead.

The street door slammed and a girl's voice called out in the hall.

Mum began to defend Albie and told Norris that she was sure he was wrong, that Albie would never get mixed up in anything funny and it must have been Nicky's own idea to go on the march. Mrs Turner told Mum to get stuffed and Mum said there was no reason to be like that and Mrs Turner said, well, what reason *do* you need? Norris Turner tucked his head back into his chest and began to massage his neck again with fingers with rings like knuckledusters on them.

A girl came into the kitchen, Ginger.

Ginger was Nicky's sister. She was chunky with furry short cropped hair. She wore her usual jeans and boots and had her shirt sleeves rolled up to reveal twin skull tattoos on either wrist. She called Albie a bastard and Albie made a dash for the door. He just about saw her picking up the knife from beside the bread bin as he threw the street door shut behind him.

Ginger was squat but she was fast. She was almost up to him by the time he was at the end of the street. "You want to stop and talk about it?" he shouted over his shoulder. "You want to risk it?" she replied and waved the carving knife about her head like a cutlass. Albie put a spurt on.

Albie had fondled Ginger one hot summer afternoon in the back row of the ABC cinema in Mile End. He'd never really fancied her but they'd gone along in a group. Nicky was there with a girlfriend and was massaging her stomach in such a way that made her yelp small yelps. Albie had seen the film before, a Michael Caine spy thing, and not wanting to feel left out had tried putting his arm around Ginger to investigate the bumps that hadn't been there the summer before. She'd responded by squeezing his balls tightly between her broad fingers, and with a relentlessness that couldn't be mistaken for passion.

Albie manoeuvred some dodgy corners round the backstreets as Ginger began to fall back, still shouting at him all the time. He'd shaken her off, for now at least. He unconsciously ran a hand up the front of his jeans and counted himself lucky.

Albie smacked the "up" button and the lift came almost immediately. Once inside, he leapt up on his toes and punched the ceiling, but the square outline of the emergency door didn't budge. Then the lift stopped. When the door opened an old lady stepped in. She was cautious and scared and eyed Albie as if she didn't know him, even though she'd kept him regularly supplied with fruit bon-bons throughout his childhood years. Albie moved back a step. He didn't want to frighten her. She was only going up a few floors to visit a friend. Albie smiled and stared blindly about him. He remembered what Nicky had always said about these lifts being coffin-shaped so that the undertakers didn't have to stand the coffins up on their ends when they brought them down. That way, the bodies wouldn't buckle up at the knees. The old lady got out.

With Albie's next jump the square in the lift roof moved. With the next it was dislodged completely and he began hauling himself up and out on to the roof of the lift. Once up there, breathing heavily and wiping the sweat from his brow, he slammed the lid of the tin box tight, and just in time too. It stopped and he heard people shuffling in, complaining about how they had to carry their rubbish bags down to the bins because the chutes were blocked again. The people in the lift were oblivious to Albie's presence, crosslegged and grinning, just above their heads.

It was years since Albie had come up to this secret place; he used to come here with Nicky. He was surprised he could still squeeze out through the hole. One kid they knew fell off the back once where there was a gap because he'd been glue-sniffing. Dead, of course.

It was dusty and dirty here. Machinery loud. Going bang-bang-bang. Scrunching wheels and weights. Warm and sticky here. Up and down like a whore's drawers, says Nicky. A laughy place here, a naughty place here. Going up and down and Albie lies on his back. He sees that it's still there. Going up and going up. *It's still there*. Nicky spraypainted it all those years ago. Have to wait till you get up close to read it. Spraypainted on the roof of the lift shaft as high up as you can get, GOD NEXT FLOOR.

After midnight Albie climbed back through the hole, down the hatch and out at his floor. His face was coal-miner black with lift-shaft dirt. He stared at himself in the bathroom mirror. His face was black in the way faces get in Tom and Jerry cartoons where people get blown up and it doesn't hurt a bit. But that was in cartoons. Mum knocked lightly at the bathroom door but it was a long time before he heard her soft voice call to him.

"Albie, I know it's a terrible thing to say, a *terrible* thing to say, but I'm glad it wasn't you."

Glad it wasn't him! Glad it wasn't *him*! What a stupid thing to say. Albie wasn't going to die. Oh no, no, pal. Count me out of that one. Do what? Leave it out, John. No way, mate. Not never. Give over. Come off it. Give us a break. Do me a favour. Clear off. On yer bike. Gertcha!

When he was younger, Albie used to play dead on the sofa, draped in a variety of poses, fingers pointing upward all stiff and twisted like dead GIs in the films. It was quite all right if you got shot by a Jap while you were fighting for your country – didn't hurt a bit. Lie there, lie there very still on a silent, summer afternoon, a murmur of traffic in the distance, watching the shadows move across the walls. Lie there very still and very, very quiet. Is this what being dead is like? Can the dead peek out from beneath their eyelashes and see the world still turning?

Albie looked in the mirror. You were all right if you could still see yourself. You must be alive. But don't take your eyes away, not even for a second.

Chapter 5

Wet light seeped in through Albie's bedroom window, the sparrows sang and Mum came in to wake him. She put a cup of tea on the bedside table and nudged him, just a little. "Wake up, Albie," she said, and went out again.

Albie got up automatically, his eyes half closed. He washed his face and hands, still grimy from the previous night's visit to the lift shaft.

"*Do* get a move on, Albie," called Mum's voice again.

The morning was a grey crayon colour smudged dirty. Albie looked out across the rooftops and opened the window to breathe in the damp air. He felt so tired. He looked at the clock. Seven-thirty. He wondered why Mum had woken him up this early. Then he remembered.

"Blimey," he said aloud, "I'm supposed to be going to work."

It was one of those Job Training Scheme thingies. The woman down the DHSS said that as he had been signing on ever since he'd left school he should go on a scheme. The money was the same as the dole but it meant you got to learn a trade. The woman said that everybody was on these schemes because there weren't any real jobs. They sign you up with a proper firm, though. And once you'd done a period of training you could go off and get a proper job with proper money. But there ain't no jobs, he reminded her and she said, of course there weren't, otherwise there wouldn't be these bloody schemes, would there? Albie figured that it might be better than sitting at home watching the kiddies' programmes all day. There were a variety of things to do. What happened was that a firm took you on and trained you alongside the normal workers.

"What about electronics?" the woman had asked.

"Well, what about them?" he'd replied.

Albie didn't want to be late for his first day of work at Planet Radio Repairs so he left home early. He was there forty minutes too soon. The door was locked.

It was drizzling miserably and he pulled up the collar of his raincoat. He was standing in an open yard full of odd scrapped bits of amplifiers, circuits and soggy cardboard boxes. A NO TRESPASSING sign hung on one of the gates but he'd been able to walk right through because they were ajar. The rain had made a puddle in the centre of the cobblestone yard and there must have been some oil mixed in it because it was velvety and threw off colours.

There was no shelter anywhere. He turned his face upwards to see where it was all coming from but he couldn't see that far. The raincoat had been Dad's when he had been alive. There was fluff in the corners of the pockets and Albie rolled it into little balls with the ends of his fingers. Everything was dry and warm in the pockets, just like the tight envelope of sheets he'd been loathe to leave that morning.

"You've found the right entrance, then," a young man shouted from across the yard, "there is another way in but that's for the bosses, not the workers." The young man came in through the gates, pulling them wide open as he did so.

Albie smiled because he couldn't think what else to do.

"You're the new JTS kid, aren't you?"

Albie supposed he was.

The young man pulled a bunch of keys out of his pocket. A couple of bus tickets flew out too. "I'm Denny," he announced. Inside, he rammed a plug into a wall socket and the whole place lit up. "Wilf is the foreman here," he said, "but we don't take any notice of what he says."

Workbenches in the large space were littered with bits and pieces of half-repaired radios. There were rows and rows of shelves round the walls. They stretched all the way up to the ceiling and were straining under the weight of hundreds of broken stereos, transistors and twisted antennae awaiting their turn for resurrection. In one corner some space was given over to a couple of small rabbit-hutch offices.

Denny showed Albie how to clock in.

"Tea?" asked Denny.

"Please," Albie answered, rubbing his cold hands together.

"You'll find a kettle in there," Denny told him, pointing out a filing cabinet in one of the rabbit hutches. "You might have to nip out and get some fresh milk, though."

Suddenly, people started to stream into the workshop. It was seconds before nine. There were a few stares in Albie's direction that lasted until they hung their coats up. "Oh, I do love Mondays," said one with an explosive clap of hands. Another unrolled a *Daily Star* from his jacket pocket and slapped it down on his work surface. A tall stooped man came up to Albie.

"New lad, eh?" He shook his head. "Very good to see new blood around, show this bunch of layabouts what real work is, eh?" He emitted a laugh that could easily have been a cough. "My name is Wilf. I'm the foreman round here, but don't take any notice of what I say."

Wilf the foreman told Albie about the firm's work, the things that Albie would be expected to do and the responsibility they all had in upholding the nation's economy, about lunch breaks and the loss of his father's leg in the trenches at Verdun. He told him about the glorious carrot of wage differentials, the ever-rising standards of the common working man and then nodded towards the filing cabinet. "Cup of tea would be nice, eh?"

Denny pointed out the rest of the lads to Albie. But the names didn't even go through one ear. Albie made them all their morning tea. "Thanks, Alan," said one of the workers to Albie as he was handed a steaming mug.

"My name's Albie," Albie told him.

"But it was Alan last week," said the worker.

"Alan was the last JTS," someone else shouted across.

"They all look the same to me," said the worker, sipping the tea Albie had given him.

That morning Albie also swept between the benches, went round to the tobacconist to get a dozen assorted fag brands and spent forty minutes in the lavatories sitting on a moist toilet seat staring up at the rain-pelted square of window. He watched the clouds blot out all remains of a watery but hopeful sun. He lit up a fag. He'd never smoked before but this seemed as good a time as any to start.

Albie wasn't used to lunchtime drinking and as he stepped out of the pub doors with Denny he realised that he was pissed. The rain had stopped but the streets were wet and mirrored the sun so that Albie had to blink. "That's a nice-looking girl in reception," he said to Denny.

They arrived back at Planet Radio Repairs. "You like the look of Tina, eh?" said Denny. "Listen, nobody starts work proper for a few minutes. We'll go and have a chat with her, eh?" He darted through the workshop with Albie behind and thumped up the stairs in his heavy workboots into the reception area.

Tina was filing her nails.

"Hello, Denny," she said without looking up.

"I thought I'd introduce you to our new JTS lad, Albie."

Tina looked up and smiled, tossing her red hair out of her eyes.

"We were just coming out of the pub," Denny continued, "and he told me he fancied you."

Albie felt like he'd burn to a crisp.

"Go away, Denny," said the girl. "Look, you're embarrassing him, he's gone bright red."

The outside door opened behind them and the bearded, rotund figure of Ray Ball, director of Planet Radio Repairs walked unsteadily in. He was waggling a rolled-up newspaper like a truncheon. "Drunk again," said Denny under his breath.

"Good afternoon," he called out, puffing on a Panatella. "And what's this? A visit from the works floor? Not a delegation, I trust. Or are you forming an exceedingly small picket line?"

"Afternoon, Mr Ball," said Albie. "We were just on our way back downstairs."

"Ha!" cried Ball. "I can tell it's your first day, lad," he said to Albie. "It's good to have you aboard, it really is. It gives me a warm feeling deep down inside to think that through my tireless work in building up this company, I'm now able to offer lads like yourself a helping hand; not that the bloody socialists appreciate it, do they?" He guffawed loudly.

The director turned his attention to Denny. "I think it would be good if you took young Albie here under your wing. You're a good worker. Show him the way."

"It's a pleasure, Mr Ball," said Denny, smiling.

"Then get to it," Ball shouted, laughing some more and waving the newspaper in the air. He asked Tina to fetch him some coffee and staggered away to his office.

Denny blew Tina a kiss as he and Albie descended the stairs to the workshop.

"You and Ball seem to get on well together," said Albie.

Denny turned to Albie. "I hate his guts," he said.

Albie was stunned. Danny explained: "A job's a job, Albie. I tell myself that I'm really a mole here, burrowing away under Ball's chair in the hope that one day he'll fall through the floor."

In the workshop, Albie was accosted by Wilf the foreman with a dustpan and brush and told to get on with some tidying up. While he swept between the feet of the irritated workers, Albie became vaguely aware of shouting which got louder and louder. When Ball appeared in the workshop it was obvious who had been doing all the yelling.

"You bloody Judas," he cried, walking slowly towards Albie. He was waving in front of him the afternoon edition of the *Challenger* newspaper that he'd brought back with him from lunch. "I invite you into my company with the best intentions in the world and on the very first day I discover your true colours – red!"

Ball shoved the front page of the *Challenger* newspaper into Albie's face. The headline was CIRCLE SQUARE BOY'S CRIMINAL PAST. Beside it was a giant photo. Formed in a thousand black and white dots, the images of Nicky and Albie stared out at an unexpected audience of millions. On a bleak wasteland Nicky was waving a mallet above his head while Albie threatened the photographer with a machete.

Chapter 6

CIRCLE SQUARE BOY'S CRIMINAL PAST.
EXCLUSIVE REPORT from JACK GAUGHAN.

Yesterday, I tracked down Albie Brownslow in the bar
of a tough waterfront pub in the East End of London.
This young man is currently at the centre of the *Boy
Dead in Circle Square Riddle*. Albie Brownslow was
Nicky Turner's "best mate", yet when I encountered
him he was swilling beer in an afternoon drinking
session the very day after Turner's death.
Hard stares greeted me as I entered the smoky, airless
bar and I was forced to pay out for drinks before I was
granted an audience with this small but muscular
cockney. Albie Brownslow was holding court with
friends and associates. He recalled his past relationship
with Nicky Turner and their crooked "capers" in this
part of town where street fights and gangland slayings
are commonplace.
Because of the forthcoming inquest I cannot relate all
the grubby goings-on talked of in that smoky
atmosphere but I can reveal that illegal activities
involving sums of money and handicapped children
were described which should make even the roughest
member of this tight-knit dockland community sick to
the stomach.
Albie Brownslow was one of the last people to see
Nicky Turner alive and he could hold the key to his
death. Was he with Turner when the tragic accident
occurred? "No Comment." Was he himself a

participant in the violence? "No Comment." Was he claiming that Nicky Turner was a victim of so called 'police brutality'? "No Comment."

I can assure *Challenger* readers that no money was given for this "interview", but it did cross my mind that it might be cash Albie Brownslow was holding out for. Both Turner and Brownslow grew up in an environment where strangers are barely tolerated or spoken to.

But despite Brownslow's silence the truth must come out about Nicky Turner's death. We can only hope that investigations will not be hampered by the loony left who now operate in this once thriving dockland. It did not strike me, however, that Albie Brownslow is a person with any particular political convictions. So one more question hangs ominously in the air. Just what were Brownslow and Turner doing on that demonstration march?

I was eventually ordered to leave. Before I retreated, however, I learnt that the two young men had both been regular supporters of a football club with a reputation for crowd violence.

We should ask ourselves this. Could it be that the new restrictions on public marches, considered Draconian by some, don't go far enough? Should there be a *complete* ban on all such troublesome events?

Chapter 7

A man was waiting to get in as Albie got out of the lift at the ground floor. As the door rumbled shut Albie heard the man say, "Commie bastard".

Walking out into the bright chilly morning Albie noticed a young man with a camera sitting on a low wall that surrounded the estate, looking idly at a fenced-off slab of tarmac. It was there for kids to break milk bottles on but vandals sometimes used it for football.

"Over here, you wally," called Albie.

The young man jumped up and raced across to Albie clicking and clicking. He snapped a whole reel of Albie full face with the tower block as background. Albie stood still for him while he did it. "Thanks, pal," the man said and ran off.

When Albie had been given the sack from Planet Radio Repairs the week before he had emerged from the workshop to be confronted by a mob of squabbling journalists out for pictures and a follow-up story to the *Challenger* item. The next day's papers carried pictures of him legging it down the road to get away from them and quotes from Ray Ball which made it sound as though Albie had been sacked for disrupting life at Planet Radio Repairs. So let them take photographs if they wanted to, was now Albie's attitude; he had nothing to hide.

Since Nicky died, Albie might have been living in China. The landscape was different and nobody spoke the same language anymore. Since the newspaper stories, everybody round every corner knew who he was. Every conversation he overheard was about him. He'd never seen so many doorways, so many holes in the walls for people to lie in wait. People were tigers.

Albie walked the windswept waste between the tower blocks. The ground was spattered with trash tossed from on high: gutted tins, fractured eggshells, rags and bags crammed with what looked like old men's guts. Albie felt as if a tornado surrounded him, like the winds that circled the blocks, carrying with it people and words that plastered themselves to him like so much litter. A copy of last week's *Challenger* flapped mockingly on the ground. A face. A machete. He picked it up and crumpled it into his pocket.

Albie took a bus to Fleet Street where all the big papers were produced – all those that hadn't moved to the new dockland sites. Albie went to look at heads. He'd been looking at heads a lot since Nicky died and had decided that heads were *nothing*. Heads were no protection against anything. He looked in at The Punch Tavern. It was stuffed full of heads. But not the one that he was looking for – a head wearing a little leather cap with wispy hair crawling out from underneath.

Albie made his way further along the street, hoping to visit all the Fleet Street pubs before the end of the lunch break. He just couldn't stop thinking about heads and he found himself constantly moving his hand across his scalp. People were all eggmen, walking around with thin crackable heads that would spill out brains if you so much as waved a spoon at them. What if a slate fell off the *Daily Telegraph* roof right now? What if a window cleaner dropped his bucket on Albie's head? What if a wing fell off a passing aeroplane, what if... what if... It was all too much to think about.

Albie had almost given up his search when he realised that he had just walked straight past a man in a leather cap. Jack Gaughan was strolling the other way; he had not even noticed Albie. Spinning round, Albie lashed out at the back of Gaughan's leather hat with his rolled-up newspaper. The man turned, obviously shocked. He was quick to regain his composure. ''Albie,'' he cried, ''I've been *desperate* to see you. I can explain everything.''

Jack Gaughan took Albie to a public lavatory deep beneath Fleet Street. At the bottom of the stairs he turned to Albie. ''Don't let anybody know about this, will you?'' He knocked on the attendant's door. A beat-up heavy-weight opened up, a punchbag of about sixty who was more likely forty-five. He was displaying a double portion of cauliflower ear.

Jack Gaughan said, ''Go and buy me a packet of fags will you, Cyril? Take your time about it. Here's a fiver. Keep the change.'' The huge man smiled, one eye closing as he did so. He crumpled the note in his fist, wrapped a coat about him and hauled himself up the twisty stairs. ''Oh, what brand, Mr G.?'' he called down from halfway up. ''Any you like,'' replied Jack Gaughan. ''I've given them up.''

Jack Gaughan beckoned Albie into the small, brightly lit room. He sat down on its one chair leaving the radiator for Albie to sit on. ''I call this my second office,'' said the journalist, leaning back and plaiting his fingers over his belly. ''With the circulation war the way it is at the moment I like to keep my informants secret, even from the other hacks on my own paper. I interviewed Tom Poppy the gangster down here, and that Broadmoor escapee. The last time I was here was for the true life kiss and tell confessions of Tutu Morrow, the Isle of Mustique model.'' He paused for a second. ''Yes, caused quite a commotion down here, she did.''

Through a small window, Albie could see a row of men at the urinals. He guessed it was so the attendant could check that there was nothing going on, or coming off, that shouldn't be.

"What's all this rubbish you wrote?" said Albie, tossing the crumpled tabloid on to Jack Gaughan's knees. It unrolled to reveal machete-waving Albie with mallet-carrying Nicky beside him.

Jack Gaughan laughed. "Albie, you're not going to tell me you think *I* wrote this, are you?"

Albie wasn't going to tell him anything.

"Sure I wrote a piece about my interview with you, Albie, but you've got to realise that writing for the *Challenger* isn't like having your own John Bull printing kit. The editor ripped my original copy to shreds and stuck in all that rubbish about football violence. I was as horrified as you when I saw it. I'm going to hand my notice in over this."

"You must think I was born this morning," said Albie, jumping down off the radiator. "That bloody story got me the sack. I've had my picture in all the papers and reporters camping outside my front door. The neighbours have all stopped talking to me, all my old mates have stopped calling and Nicky's family think I'm an urban terrorist. I didn't even know who you were when we met in the pub with Cobb."

Jack Gaughan stood up and put his hands on Albie's shoulders. "Albie, give me a break will you? I'm levelling with you when I say my story was changed out of all recognition. I honestly believed that Detective Inspector Cobb had told you I was going to be there. He'd phoned me from the station about half an hour before, telling me that you wanted to explain your side of the story. It's not my fault if he forgot to tell you. At least my story tells people..."

"The story you said you didn't write."

"They twist things, Albie, they distort the truth. They based it on what I wrote, sure."

Albie shook himself free of Jack Gaughan's chummy grip. There was a knock on the attendant's door. A man poked his head in. "Hey, Jimmy," said a Scotsman, "there's no bogrolls out here."

"You what?" said the journalist, squinting his eyes.

"Bum fodder, you know. There's nothing in the cubicles like."

Jack Gaughan looked about the small room. "Oh yeah, hang on." Flustered, he pulled a cardboard box down off a shelf. He split it open and pulled out some rolls. "Hang on, Albie," he said and went off with the rolls.

Albie sat in the chair, lit up a fag while putting his feet up on a desk and studied the *Challenger* article once again.

Jack Gaughan returned. "The things some people write on walls," he said.

Albie tossed his fag end into a flowery tin bin. "Look at this for instance," he said, holding the paper high. "What's all this stuff about 'friends and associates'? Cobb was the only one there."

"And me, Albie," said the journalist. "And me."

"Yeah. And you two were buying me drinks."

"Well, then, it's not exactly a lie that you were having a drinking session then, is it?"

Albie slammed the paper down, getting up. "You weaseley bastard," he said and grabbed Gaughan by the grubby sheepskin collar.

"Albie, Albie," the small man shouted. "We shouldn't fight amongst ourselves. It's us against the *Challenger*, don't you see? It's them we need to fight against."

Albie thumped him up against the door.

"Don't, don't," Gaughan shouted. "Cyril will do his nut if we muck up his room." He twisted this way and that, trying to free himself from Albie's grip.

There was another knock at the door. A Scots voice from outside: "Hey, Jimmy. There's no soap out here either. And while you're about it, the roller towels look like they could do with changing. They look like Hampden Park doormats on a wet Cup Final day.''

"Bloody hell," said Albie. He let go of Jack Gaughan and pushed round a few empty boxes before finding the soap. He picked up a clean roller towel, pushed the crumpled journalist aside, opened the door and emptied out a boxful of soap into the astonished Scotsman's arms and shoved a roller towel under his elbow. "Here." He slammed the door.

Albie asked Jack Gaughan where he'd got the picture from. It turned out that he'd got it from Cobb, one of a batch he had been given by Albie's mum. "Do you know where that picture was taken?" said Albie. "It was at a local waste ground that was being converted into a play-ground. We were there to help clear it up. We were just mucking about in that photograph. The way the paper used it makes us look like a couple of head cases.''

"Albie," said Jack Gaughan, adjusting his coat collar, "this is what I'll do. I'll write another story putting the record straight. I'll tell it just like it was, all right?''

The door opened. It was Cyril. "Didn't know if you were joking about giving it up, Mr G. I couldn't get your usual brand so I got this instead. You just have to roll them up yourself. They're the same as I smoke. Everything all right down here?''

"Yes," said the journalist, "why?''

"Well, Mr G., it's just that on my way back I saw a geezer coming up from here carrying about a dozen bars of soap and a roller towel under his arm.''

Jack Gaughan sighed. "We were just going, Cyril, just going. And yes, you can keep the baccy." He looked at Albie wearily. "Just trust me, Albie," he said. "Trust me.''

Albie paused to pick the creased-up newspaper from the floor. "Oh yeah," he said, scanning the story one more time. "What's all this twaddle about being told to leave the pub?"

Jack Gaughan stared at his feet for a second or two and then looked up. "Well," he said, "the landlord called time, didn't he?"

At the top of the lavatory steps a man was waiting for Albie. It was Denny from Planet Radio Repairs. "Saw you go down," he said. "You were a long time. You got bowel trouble or something?"

"You been following me?" Albie asked.

"Yes," replied Denny.

They walked to a bus stop together.

"What's it all about?"

"Well, Albie, it's about you really. I couldn't believe it the other week when Ball brought that newspaper down to the workshop with your face splattered all over it. Here, this is our bus."

Denny hurried Albie aboard and they found a seat upstairs at the back. There was only one problem.

"Oi," said Albie, "this bus is going the opposite direction to where I want to go."

"I don't think it is," said Denny, fanning a hand across the steamy window to make a hole to see through.

"You're being bloody mysterious," said Albie. "Tell me what's going on."

"I'm a poet," said Denny.

"A what?"

"I write poems from a working-class point of view. I'm one of a group of people moving along the same road. It's not easy for a working class person to admit to writing poetry. Being part of a movement helps build confidence."

"What's that got to do with me?"

"I was writing a poem about you when we met, that's what."

"Me?" said Albie.

"Well, about the Circle Square incident," said Denny.

They seemed to be travelling on the bus for a long time but finally Denny said it was their stop. Denny led Albie off through several back streets. Albie didn't even know what part of London they were in.

"It's like this, Albie. Through my writing I've come into contact with a lot of people and organisations dedicated to social change. It's altered my outlook on a lot of things."

"Do you mean communists?"

"I'm not a member of any party. It's just that I've found a group of people who believe in the things I realise I've always believed in anyway."

"I still don't see..."

"Don't you?" Denny steered Albie into a dark side street. "Usually when somebody ends up face down in the gutter with their head split open there's a bit of a fuss made about it. That's because that person has connections, connections with a party or pressure group who will demand answers, will know how to launch a campaign, know the lawyers to call, the journalists to rally, how to challenge the media. In short, they won't let the police get away with bloody murder. Organisation, that's what it's all about. But you, Albie, you and Nicky Turner. What are you? Just a couple of wallies - if you'll excuse the expression."

Albie didn't know whether to nod or shake his head.

Denny continued: "You've no movement or grouping behind you at all. And you've not found yourselves any supporters because nobody knows where you're coming from, where you're at or where you're going to. But now," said Denny, slapping Albie on the shoulders, "you've been found." They came to a row of tall, run-down Victorian terraced houses.

"Just one thing," said Denny, stopping outside one of the gates. "Why did you go on that march?"

Denny went to open the gate but Albie grabbed him by the sleeve. "Murder," he said. "You said something about the police getting away with murder. What do you mean?"

Denny opened the gate. "Why don't you come upstairs?" he said. "It's a bit nippy out here, don't you think?" Albie released his grip on Denny's sleeve and followed him. Denny rummaged round for keys, They were on the same fat bunch as those for Planet Radio Repairs. He wriggled a Yale into the lock and turned to Albie. "Yeah, Nicky Turner was murdered all right. As sure as eggs is eggs."

A bare lightbulb illuminated a thin hallway. Wallpaper peeled off the walls and something horrible and sticky had been spilled on the lino, making a ticky-tacky sound as they walked. Denny lived right on the top floor of the house, which seemed to be divided up into a number of apartments. They entered his sparsely furnished living room. The only light came from two small side lamps, one perched on a bookshelf and the other on a cluttered writing desk. Albie told Denny he wanted to pee. He was led to the bathroom where Denny clicked the light on for him.

"Don't turn it off with wet hands, the electricity's a bit weird."

Albie locked the door. What was he doing here? Here in a strange part of London, brought by a man he'd met just once before. What if he'd wandered, stupid as stupid, into some sort of trap? What if Denny was the type of person in the habit of luring young men back to his flat, chopping off their arms and legs and boiling their heads in a pot on the gas stove? Perhaps he'd make a break for the door when he'd peed. There was a clothes-horse in the bathroom as well. On it were at least a dozen pairs of black socks, a pair of jeans and a brassière.

Denny wasn't in the living room when Albie returned, but he could hear voices in the room he took to be the kitchen. He could also hear the clatter of pots and pans.

Denny came out of the room with a bread roll poking out from between his teeth. He was holding two plates of sausage, eggs and beans. He gave one to Albie and placed his own on the writing desk, pushing aside pads, pencils and screwed-up pieces of paper. He gave a knife and fork to Albie and pulled the roll out of his mouth. "Eat up," he said.

There was nowhere to put his plate so Albie sat down on the sofa and balanced it on his knees, picking at it cautiously. "Sorry love," Denny shouted out to the kitchen, "it won't take you long to prepare yourself some more, will it? I'll tell you what, I'll do the washing up to make up for it." Albie guessed that he must be eating someone else's meal. He'd have given it back but he'd already made a crater in the hill of beans.

Denny started to speak excitedly, cutting up a bit of sausage and shovelling a scoop of beans into his mouth, chopping and stabbing at the air with his knife. "People think the bad times were all in the past. They get told about how little kids used to get stuck up chimneys and old people were sent to the workhouse and about how grateful we should be to be born in such civilised times. But it's not true." A stab of the fork. "People should see the conditions of blokes down the mines today, crawling about in the dark with lungs full of dirt, men at the steelworks, staggering about in the steam, dirty and hot, slabs of white hot steel crashing about them. And there are men like machines, going daft on car assembly lines, screwing on a nut here, tightening a bolt there..."

47

A sharp whistle sounded in the kitchen and, mid-flow, Denny jumped out of his seat. It made Albie jump and accidentally drop a bean from his fork on to the floor. While Denny was in the kitchen he picked it up – hairy now with carpet bristles. He positioned it on the side of his plate so as to remember not to eat it.

Denny reappeared with two steaming mugs of tea. He resumed his meal, chopping up sausage, shovelling in beans, ramming down bread, gulping down hot tea but still managing to talk through it all. "Thousands, *millions* of men without jobs, queueing up all round the block for a pittance of dole, old geezers freezing to death in their own houses because they can't afford to turn the heating on, young lads who've had all the young beaten out of them – standing around outside the betting office praying for a winner."

A girl with a mass of red hair appeared from the kitchen carrying a plateful of food in one hand and a mug of tea in the other. "Blokes suffering this, geezers suffering that. That's all I can hear," she said. "What about all the women? Buried in back street sweat-shops, battered when they get home, raped in the streets and made fun of every day in the media."

"When I said men, Tina," explained Denny, "I meant women as well, of course."

Albie hadn't recognised Tina, the receptionist from Planet Radio Repairs, at all at first. She wore a stripy old T-shirt and tight black jeans. Not at all like her smart working clothes. Albie had to admit that he didn't think that Denny would have been her type at all. He was surprised and a little jealous. He didn't know what to say so he accelerated his bean eating instead.

Tina perched on the arm of a chair and winked at Albie. Feeling that same embarrassment as when they were introduced start to colour his cheeks, Albie stared down to his empty plate, realising that he must have eaten the hairy bean after all.

"Er, so..." began Albie, speaking to Denny, "you reckon that Nicky was murdered, eh? Well, fancy that." Albie was trying to steer his mind back to that day in Circle Square. But it was the thought of Denny and Tina living together, rather than Nicky, which filled his head at the moment.

"That's right," said Denny. "And there's evidence. Solid *photographic* evidence."

Chapter 8

Albie was listening to the very first *Frankie Goes to Hollywood* record. He didn't have any money to buy new ones these days so it was all down to the oldies. He was thinking about Denny and Tina. It had only been a day since he'd been taken to their flat but he felt eager to see them again. He suddenly didn't feel so bad that neither Rummy, Dirk nor Tommy with the one eye had bothered to contact him since Nicky had died. Denny and Tina had given him their telephone number.

There was a knock at the door, a hesitant knock that he thought at first might just be a new scratch on the old *Frankie* record. Albie looked at his watch. Just after nine.

He turned the record player off and poked his head out into the hall. He couldn't imagine who it might be calling at this time in the evening. A hand was rattling the letter box, the large fingers clearly visible as they stabbed at the flap. Albie pulled open the door. It was Cobb, his fingers still filling the oblong mouth of the box.

Cobb seemed a little surprised. "Can I come in?" he asked.

He followed Albie in. "Won't take long. Just a little info, that's all," he said. Entering the living room, he started to sing the opening lines to *Big Spender* beneath his breath. "Lovely woman, that Shirley Bassey, don't you think?" he said as if trying to explain his burst of song. "The Tigress from Tiger Bay, they used to call her. Still, not the sort of thing you youngsters listen to these days. No, I suppose not. Not Shirley Bassey. Mother at home?"

Cobb was looking a bit on edge, thought Albie.

Albie said she wasn't. "Was you expecting her to be?"

Cobb hesitated, unbuttoning his large furry coat at the front. "No, I suppose not," he said finally and sat down on the sofa, tucking his briefcase between his feet.

Looking down at Cobb, something stirred in Albie's mind. "Have I ever seen you around the estate before, Inspector Cobb?" he asked.

"You may have," Cobb replied quickly. "May well have done. There's a few cases I've been following up around these parts." He got up suddenly and stared out through the windows, his reflection clear to Albie in the glass. "Most people feel reassured at having a familiar copper doing the rounds anyway. Protection. That's what people want. Protection. That's what people *need*. As you can imagine, in my line of business I do a lot of night work. And do you know, Albie? Even I get frightened."

Albie just kept looking at the man's reflection, an illuminated head in the dark. "There was a case a little while ago that I was looking into," Cobb continued. "An old bloke coming home from the pub was viciously attacked. Right on the edge of the Hackney Marshes, an old man was cut up rotten for no reason at all. Wasn't even robbed." Albie's eyes flickered to the vague area over the rooftops that Cobb's thick index finger indicated. "Out there," he said dreamily.

"What happened to him?" asked Albie.

"He died last night in hospital. Heart attack. But without the shock, the trauma of the attack, he might have gone on for years. Poor old bugger probably lost the will to live. We've got no idea as yet who was responsible."

"A Hackney bear?" ventured Albie, returning to his chair.

Cobb smiled. "Funny how those stories take hold in the public imagination, isn't it? Bears on Hackney Marshes. Laughable. Most likely someone in a costume coming home from a fancy-dress party. Or some practical joker. I'd scotch that Hackney bear nonsense if I was on that case. Haven't people got enough to worry about without making things up? Such a lot of trouble round here, so much strife, rising unemployment, bad housing, vandalism. I really don't know what's to become of us all, do you, Albie?'' Cobb sat back down.

"It's all a bit of a mystery then, isn't it?'' said Albie.

"Mystery,'' echoed Cobb. "I wonder if that's the right word, eh, Albie? I'm a modern thinker myself. Deprivation leads to many crimes, I'm sure of it. No mystery there, Albie. Just cause and effect.''

"You've got sympathy then? Sympathy with the muggers and thieves?''

"Certainly not. We're all in the same leaky boat after all. I had just as hard an upbringing as the yobs round here. Worse! I think today, however, that there's a spiritual deprivation as well. As I said, I can see the causes of crime and violence but God gave us the ability to choose between good and evil, didn't he? I made the decision some years ago to become a Jehovah's Witness. People are surprised sometimes that a copper can have true faith. Stupid. In fact, I think it makes me a better policeman. God gave us the choice to choose between good and evil. If people choose good they are rewarded by God above. If they choose evil then I'm here to wring their bloody necks.''

There was someone at the door. It was Mum. "Hello, Albie. Ooh, and Inspector Cobb, too. Fancy sitting there with your coat on. Give it to me, Inspector, and I'll hang it up. And hasn't Albie even made you a cup of tea? One lump or two?''

Albie was feeling confused. "When you came, Inspector, you said that you needed some information.''

"Oh no,'' said Cobb. "Sorry if I've misled you, Albie.

52

I meant that I had some information to give to you. The Nicky Turner inquest opens in a few weeks' time. It should all be pretty clear-cut. An accident, of course.''

"Clear-cut!" said Albie. "I'd heard that there was some evidence of a punch-up. There's a photo of it or something.''

Cobb's mouth dropped open so wide that you could have tossed a hand grenade in there. He was quick to recover, though. His tones were much slower, more measured. "I went to see Mr and Mrs Turner earlier today," he said. "Lovely people. They're still devastated of course. So many problems. I only hope for their sake that this whole thing doesn't go on for too long. Haven't people got enough problems without making things up? A photo, you say. Who would have such a..."

Mum came back with the teas and plonked a steaming cup in Cobb's hands. "This all sounds very depressing," she said, "I'll put a record on." She skipped between Cobb and Albie. Cobb was staring at Albie as if he were looking for written messages on the lines of his face.

"I've got to go out," said Albie, sensing he'd said more than he should have. He didn't have anywhere to go but he knew that he'd gained some advantage over Cobb and had better vanish before he was asked any more questions. He rose quickly and made for the living room door.

"But Albie," called Cobb.

"You must tell Mum about the Hackney bear," Albie called out behind him.

Albie knew Cobb wouldn't stop him going out, he just knew it. Passing Cobb's coat which Mum had hung up in the hall, Albie's memory whispered to him again. He wondered if it was usual for policemen on duty to wear such distinctive fur coats. As he shut the front door behind him the strains of Shirley Bassey singing *Kiss me, honey, honey, kiss me* filtered out from the living room.

Chapter 9

The names RUMMY, DIRK, NICKY, TOMMY and ALBIE
were engraved on the walls of the tiny wooden shelter,
but someone had thought it worthwhile spraypainting
JOEY'S A POOF, SANDRA'S A SLAG over the top. Albie
sat hunched in the protection of the Victoria Park hide-
away. Protection from what he wasn't quite sure. It was
still early but it was already a bright and beautiful day. It
was cold, but the sky was as blue as a holiday brochure.
Not a cloud. The park was full of kids kicking footballs
around.

Jack Gaughan's article 'putting the record straight' had
appeared in that morning's edition of the *Challenger*.
Albie had phoned Denny and Tina right away, also
mentioning Cobb's strange visit the evening before. Tina
had said that Denny wasn't out of bed yet but why didn't
Albie pop round in a couple of hours?

Albie slipped a hand into his coat pocket and pulled out
a crumpled, half-full pack of fags. Inhaling a deep lungful
he looked about him. There were kids with kites, and
young parents pushing buggies around. Not a bad place to
kill time. "Viccy" Park had been a haunt of Albie and the
lads in their younger, summer days. How long ago had
they carved their names on this shelter? Probably not as
long ago as it seemed. There were other messages now as
well. TRACY & WAYNE, ROCKABILLY REBELS,
IRELAND FOR THE IRISH, PAKIS OUT, GILBEY IS A
WOBBLER, NF.

Albie and the lads had considered this shelter to be their
own personal property. They'd play Madness cassettes on

Rummy's ghettoblaster, a couple of hands of poker, the hop, and merry hell with intruders. If little kids were in their shelter when they came along they'd just chuck them out and if it was old people they'd drive them away by climbing on the shelter's rickety roof and gobbing down at them from above. Little charmers.

All was quiet now save for the sound of distant laughter and a solitary barking dog. Albie smiled to himself, remembering the time when some bigger kids from a rival gang had taken the shelter over. Nicky had managed to pinch one of the park keeper's hoses. They connected it up and simply hosed out the opposition. Clothes sopping wet, the big kids gave chase. Albie and the gang ran like mad to escape but the others never came back afterwards. The shelter was undoubtedly the property of some other mob of kids now.

The dog bark got louder, and looking towards the horizon Albie could see the off-the-lead mutt and its owner, just doodles in the distance. They were coming his way and as they got closer he recognised the panting dog as Tebbit, Dirk's little Staffordshire bull terrier. The slightly overweight bloke behind it – well, it was Dirk, of course.

Albie's first reaction was to scarper. After all, none of the lads had tried to contact him since the night Nicky had been reported dead and they'd carried Albie home like a rolled-up carpet. He felt that, like Ginger, they blamed him for Nicky's death. He stubbed the fag out on the bench and looked round. There was no way he could escape without being seen so he decided to brave it out. Getting up, he strolled towards Dirk and Tebbit.

There was a flicker of surprise in Dirk's eyes but Tebbit broke into a gallop when he recognised Albie, yapping and jumping up affectionately. Albie patted his head cautiously. The animal got so excited at times that it would forget why, and then assuming that it must be involved in a fight it would bite a lump out of you. Dirk cracked the dog lead in the air like a lion tamer, the whiplash sound a signal for the dog to calm down.

"Hello, Albie," said Dirk, a wide smile creasing his round face.

"Hello, mate"

They talked a little while about Tebbit. Seemed a bloke in a pub the other day had made an offer to buy him. Most likely for one of those illegal dog-fights you read about in the *News of the World*, Dirk reckoned. They both gazed down silently for a few moments at the small animal.

"It was nothing to do with me," said Albie suddenly. "You know, Nicky getting killed." Tebbit was running in circles around Albie, sniffing and snorting.

"Look, Albie, I know that. For the life of me I don't know why you both went on that bloody march but I do know that Nicky would never have let himself be led on by you – no offence intended, pal. I just don't know what to think at all. But I'll tell you this, Albie," he lowered his voice. "Rummy thinks it's all down to you. And he's after your blood. So watch out." The dog started to whine.

Albie felt his eyes moisten but he smiled. "Stay a pal, eh?" he said, "I don't know whether I'm coming or going. The whole world's been turned upside down. Stay a pal, eh?"

"Just for as long as I can, Albie," said Dirk. "I have to think of myself as well, you know?"

Albie turned to go, risking a quick tap on Tebbit's head. "I'm off then," he said. "I'm going to see some people who might be able to help solve all this mess." He walked quickly away. The kids' football game was still going strong and a wayward kick by a young curly-haired lad sent the ball scuttling past Albie's right foot. A fortnight ago he would have made a play for it, maybe even demonstrated a little dribbling skill, sent it flying between the two piles of jumpers which were the goal posts. But now he let it pass.

Walking out through the park gates he heard Dirk shouting, "You little sod!" and turned, thinking for a moment he might be shouting at him. In the distance, Dirk was chasing after Tebbit, a tooth-punctured, deflated football between the mutt's jaws.

Albie arrived at Denny and Tina's just after ten in the morning. Denny was still in his dressing gown when he opened the door. He reached down to pick the milk bottles off the step and told Albie to follow him up. Albie noted that the garment Denny was wearing was in fact a boxer's dressing gown. Emblazoned on the back in bright colours were the words Johnny "Duke" Andrews.

The flat was a mess; newspapers and magazines all over the floor, and cups, glasses and curry-stained plates on all the surfaces, including Denny's writing desk. Denny went off to change, leaving Albie to watch Tina doing her morning exercises – running up and down on the spot and bending down to touch her toes. Her programme completed, she came across to give Albie a big hug. Albie didn't know what to do when she did that. He just sort of smiled. Tina was wearing a pair of baggy dungarees and not much else, leaving her glistening arms and slim, strong back exposed.

When Denny returned, Albie showed them the new *Challenger* article. "This time Gaughan makes out that I was one of a gang of yobs who chased him along Fleet Street, threatening to duff him up if he didn't leave well alone. I tell you, I'll kill that bloke next time I see him."

Denny looked at the newspaper.

Tina shuffled a black dress off the ironing board and

disappeared into the bathroom, taking with her a fat fistful of eyebrow pencils, lipsticks and hairclips. Denny shook his head as he read the article, occasionally chuckling at some of the more juicy slices of tabloid prose. The article mentioned that a coroner had been selected for the inquest and that a date was soon to be set for the burial.

Burial! Albie hadn't even thought of that. He was only now getting used to the thought that Nicky was dead. Now they were going to *bury* him as well. The thought of it made Albie go cold.

Tina emerged, looking decidedly glamorous. She announced that it was time to go.

"I'm sorry," said Albie, "I wouldn't have invited myself round if I'd known you were going out."

"That's all right," said Denny, "you're coming with us."

"Where to?"

"To a council of war."

Tina drove in dark glasses to protect her from the glare. On the way, Albie asked who Johnny "Duke" Andrews was. Denny smiled when he realised that Albie must have seen the name on his dressing gown and said the gown had belonged to his father who had done a bit of pro boxing in his youth. He was dead now. Albie told Denny he didn't have a dad either.

Tina explained that they were going to see a man called Pope. "He's a radical solicitor, very well known on the left," she said. "He's been involved in loads of campaigns. He only deals with cases of police accountability and deaths in custody. Occasionally he'll take on causes like this one for free."

Tina parked the beat-up old car in Wapping and they got out in front of a large converted warehouse flat. Albie figured that they couldn't have been far from the pub that Cobb had taken him to the previous Sunday. Denny bashed one of the buttons on the entryphone and barked his name into it. "Come up," a dalek voice commanded.

The door to Pope's top-floor flat was opened, much to Albie's surprise, by four small, completely nude children. From the doorway, it could be seen that the large studio flat was full of huge rubber plants. There was music too, the sad hum of a bow drawn slowly across cello strings.

The children retreated through a screen of the thick green foliage. "Daddy, daddy, daddy," they called.

Denny, Tina and Albie tracked them through a clearing.

On the other side, a tall man, in deep concentration, stood hunched over a heavy wooden table. He was studying a large map of the Circle Square area of London.

"Meet Simon Pope," said Tina to Albie. The man had one of those firm, manly handshakes that you read about in books.

Pope plucked an unlit pipe from his lips and explained that the children, two boys and two girls, were about to be bathed. As he was speaking, they slithered round on the smooth polished floorboards by his feet. Albie was surprised to see that they left no snail-like trail.

"Tina has told me a little of your adventures over the telephone, Albie. It certainly sounds like we've got our work cut out."

Albie studied the well-built man as he spoke of his interest in launching a campaign about Nicky's death. Albie thought that Pope looked a bit like a scruffy Charlton Heston, except that he was going bald and had vainly drawn what strands of hair remained across the dome of his head. Even though it was quite warm in the tastefully-furnished apartment, the tall man seemed happy in a white fisherman's sweater which he wore over a thick, check shirt, the collar and sleeves old and frayed.

After a while, the cello music stopped and a woman came into the room. She was introduced as Isabella and had long dark curly hair. She wore a long flowing dress and announced that she was going to bath the children.

As the children slithered out, the tall man set about scraping the bowl of his pipe with a small penknife. He told them that he had already written to the Home Secretary demanding a public inquiry into the death. The reply had been that as an inquest was due to start an inquiry wouldn't be necessary.

"It's all a lot of nonsense, of course," said Pope, "it's a deliberate confusing of inquests and inquiries. An inquest can only judge the *cause* of death, you see? The coroner can't indicate *who's* responsible. However," he proceeded, thrusting his pipe stem at Albie, "if we can convince the jury to return a verdict of unlawful killing, then there'll have to be a murder inquiry."

"And it could end up with a policeman standing trial for murder," added Denny.

"Exactly."

It emerged in conversation that Pope had been on the march that Nicky had died on. Except that Pope had been up the front with a couple of left-wing MPs and trade union leaders. Pope talked about enlisting these people to help launch the campaign. He said that they needed to give themselves a name, "something explosive" that would grab people's attention.

"How about TNT then?" quipped Denny, "meaning 'Truth for Nicky Turner'?" Nobody laughed.

Everybody shook their heads and made a show of racking their brains. "I know," said Tina confidently, "what about INCIDENT, 'Independent Committee Calling for Investigations into the Death of Nicky Turner'?"

There was a momentary silence. "That'll do," said Pope, condescendingly.

So they all agreed on INCIDENT.

There followed a lot of crossfire argument between them about the scope of the campaign's work, publicity events, posters and information sheets that they could arrange and which experts they could call on to speak at the inquest.

Pope told them that earlier on in the day he'd approached Nicky's family about joining in.

"Mr Turner was very aggressive," Pope told them with surprise in his tone. This was no surprise to Albie. "He even told me that he had considered taking the organisers of the march to court." Pope sucked air through the unlit pipe. "Interestingly, Mr Turner also said that he was convinced his son wouldn't have been on the march and would, if anything, have been more inclined to be on the counter-demonstration if that had gone ahead." Pope's eyes swivelled round slowly to Albie, his voice taking on a quiet but unmistakably inquisitorial manner. "Tell me, Albie, just why were you and Nicky in Circle Square that day?"

At that moment, the doorbell rang and Pope had to go over to speak into the entryphone receiver. He returned with a slim West Indian wearing a thick British Army greatcoat and a tall, red, green and gold Rastafarian hat.

"This is Elliott Ness," said Pope. Ness explained to Denny, Tina and Albie that he was a photographer for *City Lights*, the well-known events and news magazine. "We're doing a special feature next week using the pictures I took of the march," he said. "I thought it only right to let you see them first, though."

The Rasta reached into the inside pocket of his giant greatcoat. Everybody craned forward as he shuffled the shiny black and white prints out of a thick Manila envelope and on to the map on the table.

There were three shots, all from slightly different

61

angles. Albie tentatively picked one up by its corner. In the midst of a sea of police and demonstrators, one officer – a member of the Special Patrol Group – said Ness, was clearly visible standing over a young man who was falling to the ground. Each of the shots charted his downward journey. He seemed to be making no effort at all to cushion his fall. The policeman above him was obviously in motion but he was turned away from the camera so that there was only a partial view of one side of his face. His right hand – and whatever he might have had in it – was obscured. The movement indicated by the position of the policeman's shoulder might have been the action of a blacksmith striking a hammer on an anvil.

"It was obvious from early in the day that there was going to be trouble. The police changed the route at the very last minute," said Ness, indicating the map on the table, "and then once it was under way they kept breaking up the marchers into smaller and smaller groups by blocking the road for minutes at a time with SPG vans. The group that went into Circle Square were following the old route because they'd been cut off from the rest and didn't know where to go. That was how it happened."

Isabella brought coffee. She told the children to get some clothes on as she was taking them out to the park. Ness took a sip of his coffee before continuing. "The police chased them into the square. The demonstrators were scared and started to run. They had almost made it all the way across the square when an SPG van came hurtling straight towards them. They were trapped and started to go back the way they'd come. The police went berserk, lashing out with truncheons." The photos started to come to life. Albie could almost hear the screech of police vehicle brakes, the cries of panic and the pounding of feet on the pavement. "Perhaps the police thought the demonstrators were attacking them," said Ness. "Who knows?'' He waved a dark brown hand in the air despairingly.

Albie could see Pope shaking his head from side to side as he gazed deep into the prints. ''There was so much to photograph,'' said Ness. ''I've never been in such a crowd before, so full of fear.''

There was a respectful silence. When Pope finally spoke it sounded almost brutal. ''Unfortunately,'' he said, ''the photographs are inconclusive.''

The others looked at him in horror.

''You're joking,'' blurted Danny.

Pope shook his head again. ''Tell me what you see in these pictures,'' he said impatiently. ''I'll tell you what I see: I see a policeman whom we can't identify who might have something in his hand near someone whom we can't identify who might or might not be injured. In fact, as far as the coroner's court will be concerned, this might or might not be a picture of the Circle Square incident at all.''

''It's Nicky all right,'' piped up Albie. ''I've played soccer with him hundreds of times with the Whitechapel Wanderers, don't forget. I'd recognise his physique anywhere. I can tell you this as well; a person who's done as much training as Nicky just doesn't fall like that, even if they were tripped. Not unless they'd been knocked unconscious first. Also, all the time I knew Nicky I never knew him to stand down from a confrontation with anyone. He must have been hit from behind without warning.''

Pope shrugged, chewing on the tip of the pipe stem. ''I'm only playing devil's advocate, Albie,'' he said. ''Frankly I'm disappointed in the photographs.''

Elliott Ness looked furious.

''I'm very sorry, Mister Pope,'' he said, snatching the photographs back, ''but if I had known you were going to be so fussy I'd have asked them all to turn round and say cheese!''

Ness wasn't looking what he was doing as he picked up the envelope from on top of the table to put back the photographs. His half-filled cup of coffee which had been on top of it went flying. The map beneath was suddenly awash with the dark brown liquid which dribbled right over the edge and on to the floor.

Well, thought Albie, Denny had said it was going to be a council of war.

They carried on arguing until late into the evening. Albie was tired and announced that he was going home but nobody even seemed to notice. A bit much, he thought to himself, considering that he was the only one of them who had actually known Nicky.

As she was showing him out, Tina told Albie that arguing was quite normal at the start of such a campaign. It would all turn out all right. She gave him a peck on the cheek.

When Albie got home he found Cobb in the corridor. He was coming out of the kitchen with a mug of steaming coffee in each fist.

''Hello,'' said Albie.

Cobb was wearing a cream-coloured shirt with the sleeves rolled up high above the elbows. It was held together by just one of the buttons and revealed a thick furry trunk above and a wild bracken of pubic hair below. The muscular hairy legs were rooted to the hall carpet.

''Er, there were a few questions I just needed to ask, Albie,'' he said.

Albie pushed the door shut and took his coat off. Mum's bedroom door opened and she stepped out with Dad's big dressing gown round her.

''Chilly,'' she said and turned the heating on. ''Go and put some clothes on,'' she said to Cobb and spoke to Albie,

"Looks like we all need to have a little chat. Fancy a cuppa?" The telephone rang and Mum picked it up. "It's for you, Albie," she said.

"Hello," said Denny. "I'm still at Pope's. We've just heard on the radio that they're burying Nicky Turner this coming Thursday. Fortunately, the coroner is to allow INCIDENT to carry out an independent autopsy on the body beforehand. Oh, and er, me and Tina were wondering if you'd mind us coming with you to the funeral. Think you can take it?"

"I think that I can take just about anything."

Chapter 10

Albie was sitting inside the Viccy Park shelter again. It was very cold. A figure on the horizon was waving its arms about. Albie walked towards the figure. It was Nicky.

"Nicky," said Albie. "I thought you were dead."

" 'Course I'm bloody dead," Nicky replied. "They've struck my name off the Whitechapel Wanderers reserves' list. You've got to be well dead for them to do that."

They walked towards the boating pond. The ripples in the water seemed heavy and thick under the bright but chilly sunlight. "So what's it like being dead then?" Albie asked.

"It's got its bad points and its good points," said Nicky thoughtfully.

"What are the bad points about being dead then?"

"Not being able to go down the boozer with the lads, I think," he said. "Yes, definitely that."

"So what are the good things?"

Nicky thought for a while before replying. "Remembering the times you were able to go down the boozer with the lads, I suppose."

"Doesn't sound so bad then," said Albie, "if you can keep re-running your life through. I mean, how does anybody really know if they're alive at all, and not just remembering the time they were?"

Nicky turned his face to the water, watching the ripples. In the distance another figure was approaching. "Make the most of it, Albie," said Nicky. "Bad things are going to happen."

*

Albie awoke. It was the morning of the funeral. The duvet had slipped from the bed in the night and he felt cold. He sat on the edge of the bed and pulled out a bundle of newspaper from underneath. He unfolded the *Challenger* with the picture of Nicky and himself on the front. The ink had blurred where it had been folded and the area round his knees had smudged. Some of the tiny printed dots had pulled away from Nicky's face and the features were unclear. Albie was already finding it difficult to picture Nicky's face. He ran a finger across the photo and a thin film of ink stained its tip. He put down the paper and picked up a copy of the *Sun*. It was the one that featured his getaway from the Planet Radio Repairs building. The image was unclear. If it hadn't been for the accompanying story you'd never have guessed what was happening. A picture of a man? Is it even a man? Is he running? Or is he walking? Is it somebody dancing? Why is he running, walking, dancing? Why does anybody run, walk, dance? Running to meet a lover, catch a bus, escape? And dancing? Why does anybody dance? Perhaps the story didn't make it clear at all.

It was funny how you could get used to seeing your picture in the papers. He thought to himself – make the most of it, Albie.

Albie was surprised to find that it wasn't raining. It always rained on funerals in the films. There was a chill wind; however, causing Cobb to rest his palm on the top of his toupée as they left the tower block.

Albie sat between Mum and Cobb in the back of a black limo, a dark tie chomping at his throat. The car was being driven by a police chum of Cobb's. It had been "borrowed" from the force. Cobb's chums called round all the time now that he had moved in, a slap on the back here, a scotch from the new drinks cabinet there. Albie had wanted to go to the funeral with Denny and Tina, but Mum had said that it wasn't appropriate, that they'd never even met Nicky. That was true, but neither had Cobb, Albie told her. Mum had said that it was only right that Albie went with her and Cobb. They were going as "friends of the family". And did that make Cobb "family" then? Yes, said Mum, he was "almost family". Shut your bloody mouth, Mum, Albie's mind screamed, shut your gob.

They had decided against joining the gathering at Nicky's parents' place but tagged on to the end of the funeral cortège as it pulled away from outside the house. Up front, Albie could see the hearse straining under a heap of cut flowers. Like Nicky, they had done all the growing they were ever going to do. Albie relaxed in the comfy seat. He always enjoyed car journeys, especially long ones. As a passenger you could forget all your problems; you might never arrive.

The line of cars halted temporarily outside the cemetery gates while other cars crammed full of tearful people from the previous funeral streamed out. They drove slowly in, smart chunky tyres pressing the driveway gravel to produce that satisfying crunchy sound. The hired chauffeurs rushed to open car doors and people climbed out in front of the crumbling chapel which looked like an upended half loaf of Hovis. The harsh light pinpointed the water in people's eyes which collected in little troughs at the bottom rim and then burst, trickling down chilly cheeks.

Albie recognised nearly everybody there. It was like a pageant of everybody he'd ever known. It was definitely the event of the season:

Norris Turner looked splendid in a smart black three-piece suit. His wife, Brenda, who accompanied him into the chapel, wore a tasteful dark outfit with matching hat and gloves. Their daughter, Ginger, looked, it must be admitted, slightly awkward in a skirt. But even with the unaccustomed encumbrance of high heels she hobbled with good grace. They were followed by an assortment of relatives, some well known, the others only lured out for this most special of family occasions. Behind them came the chaps – the well-built Rummy, tubby Dirk and tall Tommy with the one eye, all looking dashing in their well-tailored outfits. Skilfully blending into the background, Denny and Tina stood respectfully to one side, Denny in a never-before-seen suit and Tina solemnly sexy in the dark coat and dress she sported in her role as Planet Radio Repairs receptionist. And in the distance by the cemetery gates... OH, CHRIST!

A figure immediately recognisable by his chunky white fisherman's jumper could be seen waving his arms about frantically. Albie, leaving Mum and Cobb to file into the chapel without him, followed Denny and Tina as they crunched back along the gravel towards the gates. When he caught up with Tina she squeezed his hand gently. "Everything's all right," she said to him. "You've got your friends here with you." He felt himself blush.

Simon Pope was standing with three other people all wearing thick jumble-sale coats, brightly-coloured scarves and Doc Marten boots. Each was clutching a thick pile of newspapers with *Socialist Messenger* emblazoned across the top in big red letters. Pope was shouting at another trio who were approaching along the road carrying bundles of the rival newspaper, *Socialist Revolutionary*.

"The Revolutionaries are trying to muscle in," said

Pope excitedly to Denny.

"You don't mean to say *you* brought these people with you?" said Denny, indicating the jittery papersellers. Pope explained that he had just been approached about becoming the deputy-editor of the paper. "Not that I completely toe the party line, of course," he whispered.

"Well, I think it's a bloody cheek," said Denny, "this is a time for Nicky Turner's family and friends, not newspaper flogging. You can't just commandeer his memory for the use of this or that political faction."

Pope started to explain that the newspaper would be throwing its full weight behind INCIDENT but the *Socialist Revolutionary* group had arrived by then and Pope started to bawl them out.

"Well, you lot just stay outside," shouted Denny above the squabbling and trooped off with Albie and Tina back towards the chapel. "Bloody cheek," Denny rumbled as they waited behind the group of men who seemed to be taking their time getting into the chapel.

"Yeah," said Tina, "some people have no respect."

Organ music welled in their ears as they shuffled down the centre aisle. Denny was still grumbling.

It was Albie who noticed first that the reason the men in front of them were moving so slowly was because they were carrying the coffin on their shoulders. With eyes dropping to their shoes, Albie, Denny and Tina, edged sideways into the first pew they saw with empty spaces. Rummy, Dirk and Tommy with the one eye were standing directly in the row in front. "Looks like the red army's arrived," Albie heard Rummy say under his breath.

The chapel was musty with the smell of grief. Crying was clearly audible above the tape recorded music. In the front row sat Nicky's Dad. He was all shoulders, bent over as if to shield himself against the onslaught of grief. Beside him, Brenda and Ginger were holding on to each other as if they'd been sculpted that way.

The men laid the coffin down on the bier in front of the assembled mourners as if they were preparing a magician's "saw the lady in half" trick. Nicky is in that box, thought Albie, he's passive and still, cheeks stuffed with cotton wool or whatever they used to make you look nice for your family before they hammered the nails in.

The organ music stopped abruptly and a white-robed vicar ascended the pulpit steps. "Friends..." he began.

"Jesus Christ," said Rummy from the pew in front of Albie, "I can't believe it."

"...ironic that such a mournful occasion should bring us together to celebrate, yes, *celebrate* the life, not the death..."

"Shush, Rummy, hang on to yourself," Dirk was saying. "You'll just have to grin and bear it for Nicky's parents' sake."

"...and I'm sure that you can all think of occasions when that generosity spilt over and we were given the benefit of Nicky Turner's humour and compassion."

"But a *black* vicar, for heaven's sake. If Nicky knew he was being buried by a black he'd turn in his, in his..."

"...for above all else we are the sum of our parts and when all's said and done it's the good parts we remember..."

"Calm down, Rummy. It don't matter if you're black or white when you're a vicar. You're a vicar first, black second."

Rummy bowed his head, his shoulders hunched. The vicar droned on about Nicky, whom he had never met. He called for the gathering to rise and sing "Jerusalem".

Albie couldn't bring himself to join in the singing. It wasn't the vicar's words that brought tears to his eyes but the thought of Nicky's slim stiff body filling the box at the front. Albie wanted to tear at the wood, splinter by

71

splinter, to see inside. Perhaps Nicky wasn't dead. Perhaps there had been some terrible mistake. Perhaps he was being buried alive. Perhaps they were all being buried alive. Once again, Tina snaked a hand round Albie's back to signal support and despite Mum's disapproving gaze, that was how they followed the coffin out into daylight.

A gaggle of journalists, sprawling over the bonnets of the hired limos, stopped kidding and joking when they saw the mourners squeezing out of the chapel and stood up straight as a mark of respect. Jack Gaughan, adjusting his little leather cap, smiled in Albie's direction. The strong wind tugged at their coats and made them pull their collars up round their cheeks. Clutching their cameras, the journalists trailed along at a short distance behind the crowd.

Pope was standing outside the chapel with the two rival sets of paper sellers. "You could have come in by yourself, Simon," said Denny. "You didn't have to bring half of London's activists with you."

"Listen, Denny, both the Messengers and the Revolutionaries were prepared to stay outside the cemetery gates until the CAF lot came along and refused to play ball. We had to have a presence in here if they did. Bloody poachers." Pope indicated a third group of paper sellers, looking exactly the same as the other two. They were trying to flog yet another newspaper to Nicky's Mum at the head of the mourners.

"CAF?" asked Albie.

"Class Action Faction," explained Tina.

Cobb, an arm round a tearful Mum, was squeezing out obscenities from between his teeth and there was a general murmur of discontent from the crowd of mourners.

"None of you are even dressed in black," said Denny to Pope.

"Oh, come on, Denny, that's a bit much. Not that I'm

scornful of the apparatus the working classes use to signal their grief, of course."

"Sod off, Simon."

By the time Albie and Tina reached the graveside the vicar was already chucking handfuls of earth down on to the lowered coffin and was doing the "dust to dust, ashes to ashes" bit. Ginger moved forward from the crowd and tossed a garland of red, white and blue flowers into the hole. Cameras clicked and whirred. Jack Gaughan scribbled furiously into a notebook.

The ceremony finished, the vicar indicated that the gathering should disperse. The gravediggers, fags cupped in palms, started to move forward as a noisy argument broke out nearby.

"Oh no," said Tina, and started to race towards a circle of large Gothic tombs where Denny was setting about all three sets of paper sellers single-handed, angrily trying to push or pull them towards the cemetery gates.

Pope was trying to intervene. "This is neither the time nor the place," he shouted. "Not that I'm one to cut short debate, you understand?" The journalists wheeled round, turning their attentions and cameras to what was fast developing into a fight. Denny grabbed at the papers and huge double spreads flapped away in the wind. Cobb went over to try and calm things down but in the scuffle only succeeded in getting his toupee knocked clean off his head.

"Damn," he cried, and slapped his fingers down on his naked scalp.

The crowd of mourners, confused and windblown, hurried away. The vicar was now also racing towards the combatants.

"Think of the consequences of your actions," he bellowed. "You'll ruin the ornamental flower display."

*

Ginger opened the door to Mum and Albie. "If you're selling funerals we've already had one, thanks," said Ginger.

"We'd have been here earlier," Mum told Ginger, either ignoring or not noticing the girl's sarcasm, "but we spent ages looking for Detective Inspector Cobb's hair in the graveyard. It got blown away in the wind, you see? We never did find it. And it was all because of that terrible fight. I tell you, it's lucky nobody was killed."

"Somebody *was* killed," said Ginger, "that's why we're here."

On entering the living room Mum smiled thinly at Brenda and said that she would have a cup of tea, thanks very much, but no sugar as she was slimming.

In the living room the Turner friends and relatives, some still buried in overcoats and mufflers, were drowning their grief in weak tea, thinly-sliced sandwiches and large tots of whisky. They sat snug in comfy armchairs and sighed, dabbing away tears and breadcrumbs with handkerchiefs and ruddy knuckles. A large elderly lady sat with an album of Nicky's baby photographs open on her lap. "An absolute disgrace," Albie heard her say. "More like a wedding than a funeral with all those newspapers flying round like confetti."

Everybody ignored Albie, who was, to be fair, pretending not to be there anyway. Across the room, in the brightly lit kitchen, Albie could see Rummy, Dirk and Tommy with the one eye standing together, each cradling a little glass of whisky in their hands. They were positioned in a scrum circle which filled the whole of the small room. Albie took a deep breath and went to join them. Rummy kept bursting out into unashamed sobs and was being comforted by Dirk. When he saw Albie, Rummy pushed his way past the others and made his way directly to him.

He moved his face in close, talking through the tears. "This is neither the time nor place, Albie," he said, taking deep breaths, "but you'll suffer for Nicky's death, by Christ you will." He let the words dangle in the air.

Ginger looked ready to burst as she came into the kitchen as well, not wanting to be left out. "It stinks, it stinks round here," she blurted out, unable to keep the lid on.

"Yeah," said Albie, suddenly angry, "it's the smell of death. And it's coming from you lot."

Albie left the kitchen, feeling some regret at including Dirk and Tommy with the one eye in with the rest, but they had to make their minds up about where they stood. He pushed his way through the living-room mourners. He had intended to go straight home but as he was lifting his coat from the hanger in the hall he thought he heard a noise from the room at the top of the stairs. Nicky's old room.

He replaced the coat carefully.

He turned his head very slowly, almost expecting to see Nicky up there. Quietly as a thief he started to ascend the carpeted stairs. The door was slightly ajar and from inside he could hear the sound of cupboard drawers being opened and closed.

Albie stepped inside, pushing the door wide open. He found Jack Gaughan on his knees, the leather cap pushed to the back of his head. He was crouched in front of a chest of drawers and was riffling through some of Nicky's underpants. "Take a seat," he said to Albie when he looked up, "got a proposition to make to you."

Albie was stunned. It was like visiting Santa's grotto and finding a flasher in there. He could still hear the murmur of mourners in the living room directly below. "*You*," said Albie, attempting in that one word to express all the horror and disgust he felt, "*you*. In Nicky's room. I'm gonna tell Nicky's mum and dad that you're in here. Just you wait." He made for the stairs.

Jack Gaughan grimaced, rising painfully from his knees. "Albie," he said, pushing his palms into the small of his back and stretching. "You don't think I'd be up here without their permission, do you?"

Albie's eyes narrowed in confusion.

"I'm doing a story on Nicky's background, the human interest angle. I'm writing about the sort of person that Nicky really was as opposed to all that rubbish they've been printing in the *Challenger*."

"The rubbish that you're responsible for."

Jack Gaughan started to move across the room. The peak of his cap tapped and sent spinning a small Airfix Stuker fighter plane that dangled from the ceiling on a length of fishing wire. "Blimey, you don't half bear a grudge, do you, Albie? Don't you know that I've changed papers now? I'm a staff writer for the *Daily Informer* and they've taken a totally opposite viewpoint from the *Challenger*." Gaughan sat himself down on the edge of Nicky's bed and flumped backwards on the duvet. He put his hands behind his head and sighed. "Oh yes, it'll be different from now on, Albie. You'll be the linchpin of my first article, the grieving ex-school-pal and all that guff."

Albie slammed the bedroom door shut. He walked across to the journalist and kicked the side of his shoe. "Mind the leathers," said the man. "They get enough wear and tear as it is, me pounding round all day, hot on the trail of some scoop or other."

"Get off Nicky's bed and get out of his room," said Albie.

Jack Gaughan pushed the leather cap down over his eyes. "This'll be a whole new beginning for me and you, Albie," he said lazily. "I might even get a book out of all this."

Albie felt his right eye twitch. It hadn't done that in years. Without really thinking about it he strode across to Nicky's wardrobe and pushed his hands through the pile of SF comics and old football socks. His hand emerged triumphant with its index finger stroking the trigger of Nicky's pellet-gun. He stuck the barrel up Jack Gaughan's horizontal nostril.

Albie watched the colour drain from Gaughan's face. With his other hand Albie pushed away the leather cap. The man's grey hairs were revealed to him for the first time, strands stuck to his sweaty brow. Jack Gaughan moved not a jot. He spoke like a ventriloquist, trying not to move his mouth.

"Don't be silly, Albie. Put the gun away, son." It was every line Albie had ever heard in the movies. "Be sensible, Albie. You can't do this. I only want to do the best for you."

"I've had it up to here with you," said Albie, "I'm sick and tired of playing straight-man to everyone who reckons himself to be a comedian. I'll be telling a few jokes myself from now on. So laugh, you bastard, laugh."

And Jack Gaughan did laugh, but it was an hysterical laugh. "Albie, Albie," he shouted, "the gun, it's stuck up my nose, Albie." Albie automatically tried to pull the gun away but the journalist's head came with it. Gaughan was gasping like a drowning man, twisting and shaking his head, burying himself into Albie's chest and grabbing him in a bear hug. Albie felt himself start to panic, no longer in control of the situation. The barrel popped out of the man's nostril and Albie hit him on the side of the head with the gun to make him let go. Jack Gaughan started to scream and there was blood on the butt. He slithered down Albie's legs and lay whining on the floor, his hair caked in sticky red. Somewhere a telephone was ringing and somewhere Albie's name was being called.

Without thinking, Albie tucked the pellet-gun into the waistband of his trousers and stepped out of the circle of Jack Gaughan's arms. He opened the door, surprised not to find a squad of policemen and a gang of men in white coats to carry him off. Instead, Mum stood at the bottom of the stairs with the telephone in her hand.

"Albie, Albie," she called. "It's for you. Someone on the phone."

Albie descended the stairs and as if in a dream took the receiver from Mum, suddenly aware of a deep red stain on the edge of his hand.

He didn't know what to say. He was having to learn the language all over again. Finally he remembered. "Hello," he said.

"Is that Albie Brownslow?" said a voice.

"This is Albie Brownslow." said Albie.

"I happen to have some information that may be of interest to you."

"Interest to me?"

"Yes," said the voice, "the identity of the person who killed Nicky Turner."

Chapter 11

A couple of weeks after the funeral, Albie got his job back at Planet Radio Repairs.

Denny, exploiting his pretended mateyness with director Ray Ball, had made a plea for his return. He had assured Ball that Albie was "a good kid really" and that if Albie had really been mixed up in all that left-wing stuff then he, Denny, would of course have been dead against him coming back. Ha ha. Strangely, Wilf the foreman, of all people, had been a willing ally of Denny's. Albie could only imagine that his summary dismissal had somehow irked Wilf's sense of military justice. After all, even in the trenches at Verdun you'd have received a court martial before being stood up against a wall and shot.

It wasn't so bad being back at Planet Radio Repairs Albie told himself. But he knew it was awful really, simply bloody awful. The other workers were unsmiling, demanding, rude and uninterested. In fact, they were just the same as they had been before.

Since the funeral, Albie hadn't spent much time at home, choosing to kip down on Denny and Tina's sofa rather than listen to Mum and Cobb's grunt and groan exercises in her bedroom. Not that Albie felt he could complain. For they were now husband and wife.

After his first day back at work, though, Albie felt so tired that he went home to get his head down for an early night. Coming through the door, he found that the flat had been done out for Christmas. A tree stood in a corner, draped with lights and dangling balls and the entire living room had been obscured by decorations which crisscrossed the ceiling and ran up and down the walls. Mum and Cobb were out – so it was only by chance that someone was in when the doorbell rang.

The man at the door announced that he was a policeman, one of the plain-clothes kind. Albie felt his pulse race. He was a small, dapper man with a shiny new briefcase. The clips clipped open and clipped shut ceaselessly as he pulled out and pushed in reams of annotated files and papers relating to the "accident" in Circle Square, as he put it. The man told Albie that he was eliminating people from their inquiries and inquiring about people they hadn't eliminated. What had happened on the march? Albie told the man that he'd been through it all before. Inspector Cobb was always going on about it.

"Is he?" the dapper man asked. "Tell me about it."

Albie told him about it.

"That's him up there," Albie informed him, indicating the wedding photo on the sideboard, *and* the wedding photo on the little drinks cabinet *and* the two other wedding photos that were hanging on the walls. In fact, just about everywhere you looked in the living room you couldn't help but catch sight of Mum and Cobb canoodling in the rain outside the Limehouse registry office. Albie hadn't attended the ceremony. Mum was wearing a red flowery dress – and looking decidedly chilly in it – and clutching a miserable little bouquet. Cobb was wearing his giant furry coat – and a cap, stuck on at a jaunty angle which made him look a bit like a TV racing tipster.

Since his toupee had taken off at Nicky's funeral, Cobb had taken to sporting a selection of headgear which he changed daily. Large black fedoras, cute little woolly hats with pom-poms and greasy brown derbys crowded the hallway hangers. He'd explained to Albie late one night that deep down inside he wasn't really a bald man at all. In fact, deep down inside he was really very hairy, so he

80

didn't feel it right to present a false, bald, image to the world.

The dapper man picked the gold-framed picture up off the television set and gazed at it for a few seconds before putting it back. He didn't ask any more questions. "If Inspector Cobb has it all in hand then I don't have to say anything more, do I?" he said, smiling curtly. He clipped his clips shut and left.

Albie relaxed, his pulse rate returning to normal. When the plain-clothes man had first come he thought that he might want to search the flat or something. Albie hurried to his bedroom and checked that the pellet-gun he'd taken from Nicky's room was still there. He couldn't resist posing briefly in front of the full length mirror with it tucked in the waistband of his trousers before returning it to the shoebox he'd hidden it in.

Well, he thought, you never know when it might come in handy.

Next morning, Cobb's furry coat was hanging in the hallway. Albie figured that he and Mum must have returned home after he'd gone to sleep. Albie had to make his own tea these days. Before Nicky died he never used to do anything round the house. But all that had changed. He put the kettle on and stuffed a chocolate biscuit in his mouth before going to scoop up the fresh pile of envelopes which had arrived in that morning's post. He took them into the kitchen and opened them while he waited for the kettle to boil. There were three early Christmas cards, a colourful oblong envelope in which he was encouraged to send off all his undeveloped films and a warning from the "last gentile in Golders Green". He told Albie, "Yor pal is DEAD becous of the JEWS. You are a PAWN of YID SCUM who do nothing but complane. REPENT and

RETURN to yor CHRISTIAN ways. Reject eastern IMPERIALISM.'' And he signed off ''Happy Xmas''.

Since the *Challenger* stories had appeared, Albie had been receiving mail from all over. He found it worrying that complete strangers had been able to find his address so easily. Some were ''friends'' who told him that Nicky's death was all part of a Masonic conspiracy, as was the great train robbery, the abolition of the Greater London Council and the subtle alteration to the medals on the waxwork of Prince Albert in Madame Tussaud's. There had been telephone calls as well. Some were abusive but many were on his side. All sorts of people said that they thought Nicky had been done in by the police. The funny thing was that the abusive callers thought the police had done it as well, except that they said it was a bloody good job and the practice of whacking demonstrators over the bonce should be extended.

But so far, the one call that Albie really wanted, hadn't happened. The man who'd telephoned on the day of the funeral, saying that he knew who killed Nicky and had then hung up, hadn't got back in touch as he'd promised.

By the time Albie had finished throwing the mail into the bin, the kettle was boiling fit to bust and Mum came into the kitchen, still wrapping her dressing gown round herself. She almost absently said good morning to Albie and then dumped a tea bag into her own and Cobb's cup.

Cobb was fussy about his tea. He insisted on bags when they'd never used them before and instructed Mum that she was to *dibble* the bag in the steaming water, not to stir it round or mush it up against the side of the cup. It had to be *dibbled* up and down until the already milked water turned from sickly off-white to an acceptable tea colour. Watching Mum carry out this slavish ritual, intently studying the cup for fear of getting it wrong, Albie suddenly felt a deep resentment well up within him.

"Why did you do it, Mum?" he blurted out.

"What's that, Albie?" asked Mum.

Albie braved himself, "I mean, what do you see in him?"

She looked taken aback. "I'm entitled to some sort of life, aren't I?" she said, on the defensive. "Dad's been gone three and a half years now. I'm not going to grieve for the rest of my life for him. I'm not Queen Victoria. Why, I'm nearly ten years younger than Joan Collins." Albie went to take another chocolate biscuit. "And it's not as if you haven't benefited from my marriage to Inspector Cobb either." Albie looked at the chocolate biscuit. He put it back in the packet.

"It's just that I need companionship the same as anyone else," said Mum.

"But it's not as if he's much of a companion, is it, Mum? He's always out on some investigation or other."

"What are you worried about then?" she came back sharply.

She flounced off with a cup of tea in each hand back to the bedroom. She was obviously hurt. Albie sighed. He hadn't meant to row with Mum. He went to pour some tea for himself.

But all the hot water was gone.

Albie finally got a cup of tea at Planet Radio Repairs. And as usual he had to make one for everybody else in the workshop as well. He was disappointed to find a temp in the reception area. He wondered if Tina was off sick.

Denny tipped him a wink.

"We've got some work to do for INCIDENT after we've finished here," he told Albie.

Albie said sure, but when he was being honest with himself he had to admit guiltily that he was starting to grow weary of the whole campaign. After the funeral,

INCIDENT had arranged a number of public meetings. They were usually held above left-wing bookshops or community centres with peeling wallpaper and threadbare carpets. They made the case that Nicky had died as a result of police over-reaction. It seemed that everybody who came agreed with them anyway – but it was useful for recruiting new INCIDENT members. There were soon over three hundred people signed up. Denny and Pope did most of the talking at the meetings, and Albie would be called on to say a few words at the end. But what should I say? Albie had asked. Just say what you feel, Denny told him. Talk about Nicky, Nicky and you. So that's what he did. And everybody said it was great. To Albie, it sounded like he'd stuttered and stumbled through a sentence and a half of drivel before he'd start to hear his own voice reverberating round the room and then dry up completely. But afterwards it was always, "well done, pal" and slaps on the back. It felt good. But it was starting to pall.

It was already late in the day when Wilf the foreman approached Albie. "This," explained Wilf, "is a screwdriver." Albie looked at the object in the foreman's hand. It was a screwdriver, all right.

Wilf led Albie to a tall, free-standing shelf unit up against a wall. The metal construction was already buckling under the weight of hundreds of spare parts. Wilf said that since the stepladder had gone missing the workers had been using the bottom shelf to push themselves up when they needed to rummage round. He pointed to a large boot print as if he were Sherlock Holmes explaining some vital clue to a dimwitted Watson. Albie was to screw the whole thing to the wall so that some silly bugger couldn't pull it down on top of himself. Albie found a few screws on the floor by the skirting board. They were all lengths and sizes with blunted tips clogged up with plaster and paint. He set about poking them through the holes already in the giant framework. Albie was conscious that everybody was packing up to go home and that Denny was waiting for him. He decided to whack the screws in quickly with a mallet.

Wouldn't matter anyway once they found the step-ladder.

Albie walked with Denny a few blocks to where Tina's old car was parked. They both got in. In the back seat was a thick roll of posters tied up with string plus a couple of buckets of paste and some brushes. As they drove off, Denny explained that he'd parked the car a little way away from Planet Radio Repairs in case Ball saw them and realised what they were up to.

"But what are we up to?" asked Albie.

"Flyposting," came the reply.

On the way, Albie asked Denny why Tina wasn't at work. Denny told him that she had some holiday time owing and had decided to take it off before Christmas so she could get some of the shopping done.

In Islington, Denny pulled up in a side street and they got out. Taking with them the posters, buckets and brushes, Denny led Albie to a row of boarded up shops in busy Upper Street.

"We'll stick some up here," said Denny, surveying the space in much the same way as an artist might, about to start a large canvas.

"It's a bit public, isn't it?" said Albie, watching the cars speed by.

"Well, we want people to see them, don't we?" said Denny, pulling off the string and unrolling the posters. "INCIDENT have just had these printed up. This'll get all the office wallahs driving back to the suburbs wound up." He nodded dismissively at the line of cars behind.

"Blimey," said Albie, looking at the poster Denny had unfurled before him.

At the top were emblazoned the words WANTED – FOR THE MURDER OF NICKY TURNER. And below that, in a square, was the silhouette of a policeman with a big question mark where his face should be. And beneath that in blood red the letters: SPG.

"It's a bit strong, isn't it?" said Albie, peering round him at the people in the street, fearing that at any minute one might approach them and ask what they were up to.

"Come on, Albie, we know that it must have been one of the officers from an SPG van that killed Nicky."

"Maybe so," said Albie, "but won't this get us into trouble?"

"Let's find out," said Denny, dipping a brush into one of the buckets. It was quite windy, not so much as you'd notice in normal circumstances, but once they started to put the posters up great splodges of paste started to fly everywhere, into their faces, their hair and all over their clothes. The large posters flapped wildly, wrapping themselves round Danny and Albie. All the while, Albie was terrified that the police might see them. He didn't even dare to look at the speeding rush-hour traffic. Once again, Albie had the feeling that at any moment some great weight from above was going to come crashing down on him. He automatically moved a hand to the crown of his head. Scooping out a blob of paste from his ear he wondered what he had done to deserve this. He'd shot a robin off a wall once. But he couldn't think of anything else.

Chapter 12

It was a stupid day all round, really.

It was very cold out, cold enough for snow. Everyone was saying it. The inquest was due to start in two days time just before Christmas.

The previous night, as most nights, Albie had spent on Denny's sofa, talking about what was going to happen at the inquest, what wasn't going to happen at the inquest and what *might* happen at the inquest. Recently, Albie had become aware that he spent so much time at Denny's flat not just because of the INCIDENT campaign but because of Tina. Now that she was at home on holiday and Albie couldn't see her at work he found himself popping round even more. He felt that he wanted to be closer to her, closer than the bond of friendship. But Tina was Denny's girlfriend. Albie was returning home to the tower block, turning this dilemma over and over in his mind when somebody called out to him.

"It's all been a mistake, Albie," a figure called over. "It's all been a mix-up. Nicky's not dead. Nicky's not dead."

That was how stupid it was. After all the time that had passed, after they'd *buried* the bugger for heaven's sake, there was in that moment the hope stoked in Albie's mind that Nicky really was still alive.

Stupid really.

Albie blinked in the harsh winter light. The person calling over to him was Dirk. He looked pale and miserable, his face as long as a gravedigger's spade. "Albie, Albie," he called again, "follow me." He turned and ran. Albie chased after him.

Albie found Dirk heaving for breath, propping himself against the back of an old Ford Transit with the palm of his hand. Albie thought he could hear a scratching sound coming from inside.

"What you say? What you say about Nicky? What you say about Nicky being alive?"

"It's like this," said Dirk, banging his palm against the back door of the grubby van.

The back doors of the transit were thrown wide open, whacking both Dirk and Albie on the shoulders. Dirk said: "Sorry, pal," and suddenly Albie was weightless. Four thick arms hauled him inside the van. They effortlessly laid him down on the cold metal floor and clunked the doors shut. Albie's head was uncomfortably squashed up against the crack where the doors didn't quite meet. Dirk moved round to the front of the van and the chassis lurched as he climbed into the driver's seat. The scratching sound was being made by Tebbit, Dirk's little Staffordshire bull terrier. It was in the seat in the front next to Dirk but it was scared by all the commotion and was trying to get out.

Rummy wrapped the arch of his boot around Albie's neck as the van moved off. "Yeah, Nicky's alive. Haven't you heard?" said Rummy. "It's all a mistake. He just got a slight bump on the head, that's all. Didn't even hurt. *Nobody* got hurt on the demo. Nobody ever gets hurt. It's all a myth." Ginger was standing beside Rummy, lapping up every minute of it. The dog began to whimper.

"Take the Second World War," Rummy continued. "It never happened! Your mum and dad made it all up. All that film you see on the telly, that's just actors, that is. Hitler – a cardboard cut-out. And Churchill? – he came out of a jelly mould." The van picked up speed, bouncing and rocking, obviously cutting a few corners. Albie twisted his neck ever so slightly to try and take the weight of the boot off his Adam's apple.

"Oh yes," said Rummy, "everything in the garden is lovely, nobody ever really gets hurt because nothing ever really happens. Nobody ever really dies. We just go on and on."

Albie started to feel vomit rise in his throat. The boot just kept on being there. He was aware of a roaring in his ears which got gradually louder and louder, like the call of a thousand voices. Rummy was still talking although it seemed to Albie the voice was fading. "Me and the gang here – we're just figments of your imagination. Albie, life's not really this bad. Why, you're the only person on the whole of the planet. You can't even feel this boot, can you? As it gets heavier and heavier and heavier." Tebbit started to bark.

Albie's world was starting to darken. The figures above him seemed to be standing behind a pair of dirty net curtains. Dirk, craning his head round from the driver's seat said, "Ease up Rummy, he's turning blue."

Albie's ears popped. The voices in his ears reached a crescendo, "Goal!" the triumphant voices bellowed. The van stopped.

The boot removed, Albie raised his hand to his throat. It was sore and the skin was grazed. He looked at his fingers. They were smeared and sticky. The net curtains started to lift and Rummy and Ginger came gradually back into focus.

Ginger spoke: "We can leave the van here and go straight in." She kicked the van's back doors open, her boot hammering at the rusted metal catch just inches away from Albie's head.

Dirk was waiting outside to pull him out. He steadied Albie on his feet. Albie breathed deep and raised an automatic hand to the back of his head which had picked up a thin film of grease from the floor of the van. "You didn't have to be so rough with him," said Dirk, brushing the grime and flaked rust from Albie's shirt.

Leaving Tebbit inside the van, the gang marched off towards a turnstyle entrance built into a high stadium wall. As Albie's head started to clear, it became obvious that the noise that had sounded so much like the chant of voices *was* the chant of voices. They were entering United's grounds. A face at the turnstyle nodded them in. The noise inside was overpowering, a murmuring, screaming, joyous sound which hovered just above Albie's head.

The cortège moved along a corridor, their feet sloughing through an autumnal fall of fag packets, newspapers and Coke cans. At the bottom of a set of stairs, Ginger spoke: "I'll take him up on my own, OK?" Rummy gave a curt nod and Ginger began bounding up the stairs. At the top of the flight Ginger looked round. She seemed surprised that Albie had not automatically followed her.

Albie studied the faces of these people whom he had once considered to be his friends. He suddenly realised that he knew nothing at all about any of them, as little as he knew about what he was being led to. For some reason this gave him a strange feeling of calm. "Whatever," he said, and trudged slowly up the steps. Ginger ushered him along another corridor and pushed open one of the doors leading off it.

At first, Albie thought he was facing a giant colour television which somebody had tuned in to a football match. A small red player moved across the pitch dribbling the ball with good control. A small blue player attempted a tackle but ended up coming down hard on his right knee. Over and over he rolled, clutching his shins. The crowd booed. The red man made a shot but it was well wide of the goal mouth.

Ginger entered the private box overlooking the pitch

and leaned up against one of the walls. Albie strolled in behind. A fat man was inside just hanging up his jacket on the back of his chair. He began to roll his shirt sleeves up and shot a hand out towards Albie.

"Put it there, Albie," he said. "Nice to meet you at long last. You can call me O." The man smiled. He indicated that Albie should sit in a chair on the opposite side of a small table piled high with A4 sheets of paper.

"Anything I can do, O?" asked Ginger.

O asked Ginger to get on with folding each type-filled sheet of paper in half so that it became a little leaflet. She lazily unstuck herself from the wall to come to the table.

"We've only just got these back from the printer's," O explained to Albie. "This is usually done in advance." Single dark strands of hair attached themselves to O's sticky forehead. He brushed them away, leaving a small black dab there from his print-stained finger.

O looked at Albie. "Nice of you to come, Albie. Didn't want to inconvenience you too much. That's why I arranged a lift for you. Bet you've never been in one of these boxes before, eh? I've heard you're a regular supporter. I'm always here when the lads are playing at home."

Albie noticed that O wasn't taking any notice of the game whatsoever and Ginger only swivelled an eye pitchward when the crowd exploded in excitement.

"But we didn't convene this meeting because we wanted to see you, Albie, but because we thought you might want to see us."

"See *you*?" said Albie. The half time whistle blew. "Who are you?" he continued.

"That's an interesting question," said O. "Objectively I suppose we're an organisation, a party. But subjectively..." He raised his eyes to the ceiling. "What would you call us, Ginger?"

Ginger paused in her leaflet folding. "I'd say we were

91

the spirit of England,'' she said finally.

O smiled at Albie.

''That's why we thought you might like to chat to us, Albie,'' said O. ''You're a fit young English boy. What the hacks from the establishment press have been saying about you being a vandal, a red, a criminal – well, I know it's all garbage. You should see the stuff they print about us.''

Albie looked down and idly started folding a few leaflets himself. ''As you'll know, Albie, the organisation I represent pulled out of the November march to avoid any violent confrontations,'' said O. ''Must admit though, I'm curious about why exactly you were there.'' O smiled with his mouth but not much else. There was a knock at the box door.

Ginger moved across to open the door. A group of about seven or eight young kids peered in from the corridor, hovering at the threshold. ''OK lads,'' said O. ''There's only been time to fold about half of them so you'll have to do the rest as you go along or give them out as they are.'' He started to pick up the wodges of leaflets and place them in the arms of the youths who filed past the open doorway. There were dozens and dozens of them, or so it seemed.

Albie took the opportunity to investigate his throat. The blood had congealed on his neck. It felt rough and sore. Outside they were playing pop music through the ground's loudspeakers and the crowd looked still, thoughtful even.

A few torn and crumpled leaflets and a pile that had only been printed on one side were all that remained of the large stacks that had been in the box when Albie entered. O stretched and yawned. They started to play *Happy Days Are Here Again* through the speakers. It sounded a bit curious in among all the pop records but the crackly, thin voices of the Ovaltinies brought a smile to O's face. ''I like this one," he said standing up, "it's full of optimism." The whistle blew for the start of the second half.

"Now, Albie. You're expecting me to give you a lecture on the Labour Party reds, the supremacy of the white race and the evil of the dirty blacks who go around poking their willies into English tarts, aren't you?"

Albie said nothing.

"Well, I'm not," said O. "That's all a bit peripheral to the main point. It's all very attractive window dressing to get the East End yobs into the party." His voice trailed away as he turned to survey the football match beyond for the first time. "But you, Albie, well, we're speaking equal to equal, aren't we? First off, I'd like to make it clear that the organisation I represent isn't hostile to you in the least, nor even towards the majority of these student types who go round demonstrating all the time. After all, there's enough to complain about in this country, isn't there? But the fact is that people like that have been duped into a liberal anything-goes line instilled into them by successive Labour-Tory coalitions – which is all Parliament ever amounts to. The British race has been set at its own throat by engineered splits in the social fabric."

Albie must have looked pained.

"It's like this, Albie," O folded his arms. "I don't blame the youth for our problems, or even the blacks – brought over here in the interests of international capitalist and communist conspirators attempting to mongrelise our race – it is *they* who are to blame."

"They?"

"Oh, come on, Albie. You know who we're talking about." O rubbed his index finger up and down the length of his nose and giggled childishly.

Albie must have looked more pained than ever.

"But maybe we should take this one stage at a time, eh?" said O, his voice dropping to a whisper. "I just want you to come over to our side, Albie, start supporting us when you talk to the press, tell them about how you and Nicky were *against* that march and had gone along out of curiosity. Ginger here has assured me that Nicky wouldn't have been there marching with the reds. I want you to realise your true feelings to the world, Albie, not to feel embarrassed, to tell everybody how proud you are of your heritage, that Nicky was a martyr to his race." O unfolded his arms. His voice was getting louder. He cupped his palms up and outwards. "Why not start coming along to our meetings? Represent us at lectures, talk about you and Nicky – the memory of Nicky – that's all we ask. You could be a valuable asset to our little group. You'll soon see that we're the only ones who've seen the clear straight path to Utopia, that we are the hands on the tick-tock march of time. We have seen the clockwork inside the clouds, Albie." O was shouting now. "Yes, Albie, the clouds are run by clockwork!" There was a loud booing as someone missed an easy goal. Great beads of sweat were pumping out of O's hairline. He laughed and took a deep breath as if he'd just emerged from a wild surf.

O looked at the watch on his pudgy wrist. His voice was once again that of the friendly host Albie had met on entering the private box. "Why don't you get off now, Albie? Ginger will show you out. If you wait till full-time you'll only get caught up in the crowd and you know what animals these people can be." He gestured to the football fans outside the window.

Albie got up and walked to the door. Ginger held it open for him. "Oh, Albie," O called. Albie turned to find O holding a leaflet out at arm's length. Albie took it. "A little window dressing," said O.

Albie didn't really understand the comment until he started to read through the leaflet as he walked to the exit with Ginger. An item on the back read:

Death in Circle Square survivor Albie Brownslow is expected soon to make important disclosures at the forthcoming inquest, regarding the real reason for his own and Nicky Turner's presence at the communist-inspired demonstration march in which Turner died. Alibe has met recently with a top-level party member and has discussed his ideas on racial purity and the international Jewish conspiracy and his own desires to put the record straight about just whose side he's on. Watch this space!

"I've got more scriptwriters than Bob Hope," said Albie to Ginger. "What does O stand for anyway?"

"Oracle," said Ginger.

Albie went straight round to see Denny. He wasn't in, but Tina was. "Blimey, what happened to you?" she asked, eyes agog at the roughed up vision before her.

"Oh, I wasn't looking where I was going. I walked into a fascist."

Albie told her all about it as she helped remove his bloodied shirt and bathed his neck with warm water and cotton wool. He sat cross-legged on the floor as she knelt down behind him.

"How do you think it all fits in with Nicky's death?" she said. "Do you think this O bloke is involved with Nicky's death in some way?"

"I honestly don't know Tina. Can't imagine Ginger would be hanging round with him if he was."

Tina asked Albie if he wanted a scotch to kill the pain. Albie told her he didn't drink spirits so she got some ring-pull cans of beer out of the fridge and put them down on the floor in front of him. "I've got something even better for easing pain," she said. Tina started to stick three Rizla cigarette papers together in an oblong shape. She produced a silvery block the size of an OXO cube from a drawer, and peeling away the foil, crumbled a corner of the dark brown chunk within on to a bed of tobacco she had placed on the Rizlas. She rolled it all up into a fat cigarette and lit one end. She took a couple of puffs before offering it to Albie. There was lipstick on the butt.

Albie looked blank.

"You're not going to tell me you've never tried it before, are you, Albie?" said Tina.

Albie didn't like to admit he hadn't.

A few puffs and the pain in his neck was gone. It was a strange sensation, though. He seemed to lose his concentration completely and yet at the same time every thought that his mind randomly settled on he seemed to perceive more clearly than ever before. Tina seemed to be constantly asking, "Better now? Better now?"

Halfway through the second fat cigarette Albie began to feel thirsty and he leaned forward to pick up one of the cans off the floor. The can opened with a fierce hiss, shooting out the thin spurt of beer over Tina's small breasts. She screamed a shrill scream which had turned to giggles even as Albie was mumbling apologies and trying to rub her black cotton blouse dry with the sleeve of his shirt.

"So that's the game, is it?" said Tina, sitting down in front of him. She grabbed for a retaliatory can which she proceeded to shake violently up and down in her fist. "Cop this," she said, and ripped the ring-pull back so that the beer inside shot out all over the crotch of Albie's jeans.

"You mare," he shouted, grasping her shoulders and playfully pushing her back on to the floor. Tina landed on her back with a thump and they rolled snarling and giggling on the floor. The beer cans went rolling, spilling out the foaming liquid which formed long dribbles across the floor. As they both sat up, Albie leaned forward and pushed his lips on to hers, his hands automatically curling round her, palms massaging the small of her back. He poked his tongue between her lips and wriggled it round inside her mouth. Tina twisted her tongue round his, grabbed Albie's arms and pulled him towards her momentarily before roughly pushing him away.

"No," she said, sucking in deep lungfuls of air, "no, I don't think so, Albie." She half smiled and half scowled.

Downstairs they could hear Denny coming in through the front door.

A stupid day all round, really.

Chapter 13

The night before the inquest was due to start, Detective Inspector Cobb asked Albie to take a ride in his car.

He explained that he wanted a chat.

"Where are we going?" asked Albie as they drove off.

"The Hackney Marshes, of course," Cobb replied.

Once there, they got out to stomp about in the darkness, a single beam of light provided by Cobb's torch. It was bitterly cold. Everybody was saying that snow was on the way.

"I'd stop right there if I was you," said Cobb, seeing the direction that Albie was moving in. Cobb shone the beam of the torch down to just in front of Albie's feet. There was a huge hole where a tree had been plucked out by the roots, doubtless in the great hurricane of '87. "That'll take you all the way to hell, Albie," said Cobb. The beam stirred round the hole. Albie took an automatic step backwards.

"What are we doing here?" asked Albie.

"We're looking," said Cobb.

"What are we looking for?"

"A man in a bear suit."

Albie had promised Denny that he would meet him in the pub. If only he could get away from Cobb.

"What if it's a real bear?" asked Albie.

Cobb didn't reply, he merely adjusted the smart checked cap on his head – another addition to his wardrobe.

"I never was on this case officially, Albie," Cobb said finally, "that's why I'm here off my own back, alone, at night. It's all nonsense, of course, but who knows what's behind it? There's no smoke without fire, after all."

"The marshes are a big place, Inspector Cobb," said Albie, "there's no chance of us finding anything."

"In all my investigations," said Cobb, "I like to get the *feel* of the place. I like to let things seep in. Sometimes you don't realise you've discovered something, interpreted some clue or other, until you've let it all settle in your head. The investigation never really stops, Albie. It's like the investigation into the very meaning of life itself. The quest for God, if you like. And it never stops." The beam circled the black, round and round.

Cobb shone his torch at his own face, casting smudgy shadows in all the wrong places.

"Albie," he started quietly, "the Nicky Turner inquest starts tomorrow. I wonder if you've thought about the trouble your INCIDENT mob could cause. I'm not going to tell you we're all angels but what I do know is that no copper makes it his day's work to go out and kill someone. I don't know if Nicky Turner died in a scuffle with an officer or not but I do know that even if he did it would have been an accident. All this talk of murder is plain ridiculous."

"There's no smoke without fire, Inspector Cobb."

"Who told you that?"

"You did."

"You trying to be funny, Albie?"

"Dropping a milk bottle on the floor, that's an accident," said Albie. "Nobody in the world ever got accidentally beaten to death."

Cobb looked like he was about to lose his temper, but calmed himself down and asked Albie to return to the car.

They both sat in the front seats, staring back at their marsh-filled faces reflected in the windscreen. Such was the temperature that even though the heating was full on they had to pull their coats up about their faces and sit with hands in pockets.

"This Nicky Turner business," continued Cobb in a

world-weary tone. "Don't you see that even if it's true that he was hit over the head by a copper — accidentally of course – that it would put the police force in a bad light? If it were proved at the inquest that a policeman was responsible then it would have a false importance put on it. Get my drift? What I mean is that all year round coppers are doing a cracking job, foiling bank robbers, arresting rapists, helping old ladies across the road, I'm sure you'd agree with that, Albie. And then just because of a split-second accident on just one day of the year, all that good work is forgotten. So it would be true and false all at the same time, you see?"

"I see Nicky laying out flat in a wooden box, that's what I see," said Albie, "Sellotape holding his head together."

Cobb exploded. "Don't speak like that about the dead," he barked, smacking his hand down on the wheel of the car. "Listen, I know the sort of person you are, the sort of person Turner was, and I know why you went on that demonstration march. And if you don't admit at the inquest that you were both there to cause trouble, there'll be repercussions for you and for others. If the inquest returns a wrong verdict all hell will break loose."

"What's that?" shouted Albie, looking out through the windscreen.

"Where?" said Cobb.

"A figure in the distance there. Sort of bulky. It disappeared behind that bush thing."

"Right," said Cobb and pushed the car door open. "Keep an eye out for me, eh?"

Albie nodded sharply and Cobb started to run into the distance, an index finger holding his flat cap in place. He was going at a pretty good pace for a man of his age, thought Albie. Cobb vanished into the bushes.

Albie glanced at his watch, opened the door and stepped out of the car. He walked back to the main road and looked for a bus.

It was spitting with rain as Albie got off the bus and with the collar of his coat turned up he ran the last hundred yards to the World Turned Upside Down.

He had the uncomfortable feeling that he had been followed all the way from Hackney Marshes.

As he had boarded the bus after shaking off Cobb, a car which had been parked on the edge of the Marshes had suddenly started up and had followed the bus all along its route. And now, as Albie was entering the pub doors, he could see the car parking up the road and a man in a light raincoat starting to climb out.

Denny was waiting in the Saloon bar for Albie. "Where on earth have you been?" he asked.

Albie said he'd get some drinks and tell him all about it.

"If you can get served, that is," called out Denny above the hubbub.

There was an inter-pub darts match going on in the pub and the place was crowded. The sound of arrows thudding into the board was greeted with loud cheers or disappointed groans. While Albie was waving a fiver around, unsuccessfully trying to attract the barman's attention, he noticed a blond, youngish man staring at him from further down the row of thirsty customers. It must have been raining heavily out now because the man's light raincoat was dripping. Bar regulars and darts players jostled and joggled alongside the man, who stood stationary in the midst of it all, not drinking or even trying to order.

The man slowly pushed his way through the crowd towards Albie. "Hello," he said hesitantly. "It's about this Nicky Turner thing. It was me who phoned you up on the day of the funeral. I think I know who bust open your mate's skull and how we can prove it."

Chapter 14

It was the first morning of the inquest and what everybody had been predicting finally happened – it started to snow.

Albie gazed at the silently falling flakes through his bedroom window as he was getting dressed. The East End looked all right beneath an inch or two of white. It covered up the dirty gutters, dustbin lids and dogshit. It cleaned the place up.

Albie wore his big heavy winter coat for the first time in ages. He wrapped a check scarf round his throat too. It had been his father's. He met Denny outside the coroner's court, the snow flecking their clothes and hair. Denny told Albie that the others were already inside.

Although it was plainly a modern building on the outside, Albie realised as he entered the packed court room that he had been expecting to sit in some high, echoey, Victorian chamber, dust dancing in great shards of light beaming in through tall, cathedral-like windows. But it was nothing like that. Court No. 2 was light and airy and had a relaxed comfortable feel to it. There was amplification at all the positions where people might have to stand to speak.

Albie had also imagined that the coroner would look like a judge or something, with a huge, powdery wig and red gown. As it happened, Coroner Parkinson-Kettle turned out to be a balding, middle-aged man in a dark crumpled suit, his turnups bunched up round his inappropriate Hush Puppy shoes.

''All stand, please,'' called the court usher, in a manner which reminded Albie somewhat of the chalker shouting out the scores in the World Turned Upside Down darts tournament the night before. Parkinson-Kettle entered and took his place.

Formalities were dealt with. Simon Pope stood up to say that he was representing INCIDENT and another man, younger than Pope, bobbed up and announced that he was Stephen Bradley, there on behalf of the police. He was a tall, smartly dressed man with creamy blond hair. Handsome, Albie supposed. In marked contrast to everybody else in the court he was wearing a red bow tie – a sure sign of supreme confidence.

Parkinson-Kettle began to speak in a high tense voice while rubbing at the lenses of his glasses with a grubby looking hankie. He addressed the jury of eight men and three women. This was a case which had attracted a great deal of publicity, he told them. They should try as much as possible, however, to put all they had heard, read and seen to one side. They would have to make up their own minds on the evidence presented at the inquest.

To the right of the coroner was the witness box and above that the public gallery where Albie and Denny sat. They were squeezed in very tight due to the large amount of press who had spilled out of their own gallery at the back and were shuffling writing pads round on their knees and whispering into each other's ears.

Opposite the witness box was the jury, sitting up straight and paying attention like an infant school class. The poor devils had done their best to look smart but with the sudden arrival of snow their carefully selected outfits had been forced to accommodate all sorts of supplements – men in well-cut suits had dug garish jumpers out of the closet and one otherwise elegantly dressed woman had on a ridiculous pair of furry boots that looked as though they had been lopped off a bear from just below its knees.

Putting his glasses on his nose, the coroner fixed the jury

in his gaze for the first time. His voice took on a deeper, sterner tone. All they had to do was decide who the deceased was and how, why and where he had come to his death. "You are the sole arbiter," he told them, "the evidence will be placed before you which you can either accept or reject at will. You alone will decide whether the death was unlawful killing, accidental death or misadventure."

The coroner put his arms on the desk and leaned towards the suitably worried-looking jurors. He continued: "The purpose is not to decide differing points of view between conflicting parties – the purpose is to inquire about the circumstances objectively. We are all here with a common task to examine the evidence and decide where the truth lies. At an inquest nobody is on trial."

Parkinson-Kettle called a policeman, SPG Inspector Walker, to the witness box.

Inspector Walker was a calm, open-faced bobby. He flicked a boyish nod in the direction of the jury. In answer to questions put to him by Bradley, he told the court that there had been over a thousand protestors on the march and because of the threat of a right-wing counter demo, almost as many police. The only recorded violence of the whole day was the Circle Square incident. Over thirty police officers had been injured and nearly sixty demonstrators, some with head injuries. Only one person had died.

Inspector Walker was in charge of SPG Unit 3. He explained that the Metropolitan Police Special Patrol Group is divided into units, each consisting of three vans. "As soon as I received radio reports of a group of marchers taking an unauthorised route through the square I ordered the van I was in to go there." Parkinson-Kettle was listening to the officer intently, his glasses firmly pressed on to his nose.

Inspector Walker continued. "When we got there we found that an ugly situation had developed. I could hear the sound of breaking glass and I could hear missiles bouncing off the roof of the van. There was clearly a riot in progress. I called for another van."

"How did you come to the decision a riot was going on?" asked Pope, pipe in mouth, when his opportunity came to examine the witness.

"Well, the demonstrators were running about all over the place. Some were waving their fists and throwing lumps of concrete and milk bottles."

"How many people did you see throwing missiles?" pressed Pope.

"Well, just one actually, the person who hit me with a half brick." He patted an area on his uniformed shoulder. "That's when I gave the order to draw truncheons. About a dozen of us from both vans advanced on the crowd behind shields."

"What on earth were you trying to do?" asked Pope incredulously, plucking the pipe from his lips to good effect.

"Disperse the crowd, sir."

"Were you aware, Inspector Walker, that police had followed the demonstrators into the square, effectively blocking any exit they might want to make, therefore giving them nowhere to disperse to?"

Inspector Walker said nothing. Coroner Parkinson-Kettle looked sternly over the top of his glasses at Pope.

"It's a good start," whispered Denny to Albie.

After lunch, Parkinson-Kettle started to call the witnesses. First up was a tall, distinguished-looking Asian woman. She stood, slightly haughty and straight backed in the box. Her slim fingers occasionally fiddling with a fold in her sari, were the only indication of any nervousness on her part. Parkinson-Kettle removed his glasses.

Parminder Haque explained to the court that she had been inside a hotel on the south side of the square on that day. "Outside the window, I saw the marchers enter Circle Square and then saw some police vans coming down a side street towards them from the other side. They were moving very fast. The vans stopped and I saw policemen with shields coming out. The demonstrators started running and the police chased them. I saw police hitting people. And they were pulling people's hair. They tossed some of them into police vans but mostly they just seemed to be hitting people. I saw one young man in particular. He was running away and a policeman hit him for no reason at all." Parminder Haque seemed sure of herself until Stephen "Bow Tie" Bradley pushed her on details. What hand was the truncheon in? Was the man she saw being hit dark or fair haired? Which way across the square was he running? Come on, you must be clear!

Parminder Haque added that she had seen demonstrators throwing stones at the vans – but only after the police started to attack. Parkinson-Kettle replaced his glasses on his nose so that he could peer over them at the witness.

"How long have you been in England, madam?" he asked, interrupting Bradley's questioning.

The woman looked confused. "I came in 1965," she told him, "on the day Winston Churchill died."

"You are not a tourist then," Parkinson-Kettle continued, "staying as a guest at a hotel."

"No," said Parminder Haque, "I am working at the hotel."

The coroner nodded, but he wasn't finished yet.

"Could you tell the court the nature of your work there, madam?"

"Yes, I'm currently working at the hotel as a cleaner." Her fingers pinched the fabric of her sari.

Parkinson-Kettle nodded again, satisfied now.

Albie went home with Mum on the bus. The snow had settled quite thickly and the traffic crawled. Mum was talking as Albie gazed out of the window. Everything looked so nice under a layer of white.

"Albie," Mum said, "why are you doing this, dragging out Nicky's death? It's all the fault of these INCIDENT people if you ask me. What's it got to do with them? It's killing Brenda and Norris. They just want to forget all about it and rebuild their lives. Let the dead rest in peace, Albie. You can't bring back the dead, you know?"

Albie said nothing.

"And after all, Albie," added Mum, "everybody dies. Are you listening to me, Albie? I said, everybody dies."

Up close, Detective Sergeant Starling didn't look as young as Albie had first thought when he'd approached him at the bar of the World Turned Upside Down. He was slim and lithe but tiny crow's feet reached from the corners of his eyes to his straw blond hair which you might even have thought was dyed unless you knew that policemen didn't do such things.

It was early morning and Starling sat in a solitary ray of cold sunshine which shone in through the window of Pope's cupboard-sized office. He sat with his legs crossed, almost elegantly, and his hands in his pockets. Round him stood Denny, Pope and Albie. On the walls were framed documents saying what a clever boy Pope was.

Denny checked the ID in the small leather wallet. "OK," he said to Starling, "so you're a for-real policeman. I believe you. That's why I'm wondering what you're doing here."

"Upholding law and order. That's what I'm doing here. That's what I do everywhere," Starling replied. He was sitting very still in the hard wooden chair.

"I must say, we're very grateful that you've agreed to meet us," said Pope, pulling his pipe from his jacket pocket and waving it about theatrically. "Your input could have a very great impact on the course of this inquest."

"Oh sure," said Denny suddenly and loudly, "our friend Starling here could take us on a course all right – straight up the garden path!"

Pope appealed to Denny: "Look Denny, I think we're going to have to take Detective Sergeant Starling at face value. I'm all for healthy cynicism but..."

Starling laughed and unfolded his legs. "Oh, come on, gentlemen," he said. "You don't have to play Good Cop and Bad Cop for me. I know it already. If I'd have wanted amateur dramatics I'd have gone to the local church hall. I'm here to let you into a few secrets. If you're not interested then neither am I."

"We're interested," said Pope. "Why are you?"

"I'm an old-fashioned copper. When members of the public end their lives face down in the gutter with their skulls split in half I like to know who did it."

"OK," said Denny, "a copper whacked Nicky Turner on the head and killed him. And you're going to tell us who it was."

Starling shifted in his chair. "I'm feeling a lot of aggression here, gentlemen. I feel that my contribution isn't really wanted."

"A drink?" suggested Pope.

Starling sat silent.

"Scotch?" offered Pope.

"I'm teetotal," said Starling.

Pope pressed a button and spoke into a square box on

his desk top. Everybody sat down, the space was so small that people had to work hard at not letting their knees touch.

"So what happened on November 5th then, Inspector Starling?" asked Denny, "besides people letting off a lot of rockets that is."

"On the actual demonstration, I don't know," replied Starling. "What I do know is that the first Unit 3 van to be sent into Circle Square was signed out in the log book as having six officers on board, Inspector Walker and officers Green, Rivers, Currie, Hayter and Baylis. I was at the Central London station when they were checked out. Later on in the afternoon after Nicky Turner died, I was asked to make a copy of that list. It's just a sheet of paper that fits into a loose-leaf folder. The names Green, Rivers and Currie had all been whited out and replaced with the names of three other SPG officers who hadn't been within a mile of Circle Square that day. If you looked in the log book for that day's record now you'd find a photocopy of the altered document, not the original."

"Are you often asked to do secretarial tasks, Detective Sergeant Starling?" asked Pope, sucking on his unlit pipe.

"Never," said Starling, "but the Detective Inspector who asked me to do it wasn't based at our station and didn't know where our photocopy machine was kept. I was shocked when I found out later the implications of what I'd done."

"But why should anybody want to alter a document?" asked Pope.

Starling laughed.

There was a hesitant knock at the door and a young girl brought in a tray with four teas, sugar and a jug of milk. As Starling sipped at the tea, Albie noticed that the policeman wasn't the calm, still figure he seemed to be. A very slight tremble ran up and down his whole body.

His apparent cool came out of a constant attempt to keep this in check.

"I find it incredible," said Pope resuming the converstion with Starling, "that a DI from another station was allowed to come in and rummage through SPG files."

"Foolishly, I'd assumed that he had been sent to investigate the unit because of the riot. He spoke to others in the station, of course, before the death was confirmed but if you think anybody else is going to admit that..." Starling spread an expansive hand.

Pope jabbed the pipe stem in and out of his mouth. "It's not even as if one of the SPG officers involved had a direct hand in what you allege," said Pope, "so what's the motive? What's this DI's interest? We need a provable link."

"What's the DI's name anyway?" asked Denny.

"I didn't catch it. I only glimpsed his ID," said Starling sipping the last of his tea, "all I remember about him was that he was wearing a really obvious toupee."

Chapter 15

The inquest resumed that afternoon with the evidence of a young woman called Pru Scott who had come forward the day after Nicky had died. She had spoken with him in Circle Square itself. Albie liked what he saw when he saw Pru Scott. He liked it a lot. She was the only person Albie had ever seen who could make a duffel coat look sexy. She was small and blonde and had a CND badge pinned to her beret.

"Ms Scott," began Pope, "had you ever met Nicky Turner before the day of the protest march?"

She said she hadn't, a slight tremble in her voice. "He didn't seem to belong to any of the participating organisations. He just sort of tagged alongside the group I was with and started talking to me." She giggled nervously, "Actually, I think he was trying to chat me up."

There were a few chuckles from the press gallery and Pope thought he'd help Pru Scott with a fatherly smile. She explained how they had all taken a wrong turning into Circle Square.

Pope began to run the mouthpiece of his pipe across his bottom lip. "Tell us what happened once you were in the square," he coaxed.

"It was horrible. As the police started to charge I jumped into the doorway of one of the hotels at the side of the square. The police were lashing out all over the place. I was afraid of being hit."

Coroner Parkinson-Kettle sighed audibly at this point and removed his glasses, an action which he performed whenever anybody said something he didn't want to hear.

Pru Scott continued regardless: "I saw Nicky Turner being hit by a policeman. Only it didn't look like he was using a truncheon. It looked like something smaller."

There was a hum within the court. The coroner had to shush the press gallery.

"I was scared but I found myself running over to the policeman. I said something stupid like, 'Why don't you pick on someone your own size.' He looked at me like I was crazy."

"What happened then, Ms Scott?"

"He hit me as well."

The small blonde girl went on to explain that she was taken to hospital in the same ambulance as Nicky. "He looked in a really bad way. His eyes were rolling about all over the place and he kept mumbling unintelligibly. At the hospital they put him on a stretcher. He vomited then. It looked like blood and water." When her head had been dressed she'd made enquiries about Nicky and had been told he was dead. Then she'd told a policeman at the hospital she'd seen him being hit.

Bow Tie Bradley sprang to his feet to put some questions to the young woman.

"When Nicky Turner approached you for the first time Miss Scott," he said, "what sort of mood was he in?"

Parkinson-Kettle replaced his spectacles for Bradley's questioning. He screwed his eyes up and stared at the girl as if she were something pinned beneath a microscope.

"He was talking nineteen to the dozen so I guess he was nervous," she told the court. "I got the impression he'd never been on a demonstration march before."

"Tense?" said Bradley.

"Nervous," said Scott.

Bradley was the most patient of inquisitors: "About the period you spent in the hospital," he purred sympathetically. "Were you possibly disorientated by your injury and the general confusion of the situation?''

Pru Scott told him that wasn't the case. But she's said no to Bradley just once too often. And people like Bradley didn't like being spurned and didn't have to put up with it. His voice hardened. ''The police report I have before me, Miss Scott, indicates that when you spoke to the officer at the hospital about Nicky Turner you told him that you 'assumed he had been hit by a policeman', a little different to saying you'd seen him actually being hit, eh Miss Scott?''

Pru Scott looked stunned. ''No, no,'' she insisted, ''I definitely told him that I saw a policeman hitting him. I did, I did.''

But the damage had been done.

As Pru Scott stepped down from the witness box, Denny told Albie that the police report Stephen Bradley had referred to had been compiled by Commander Powell. The coroner and Bradley had copies but INCIDENT had been denied access by Parkinson-Kettle. Denny pointed out Commander Powell in the court room. It was the small dapper man who had visited Albie at home just before he'd started back to work.

On their way out of the building, Denny asked Albie at which point he'd been separated from Nicky on the march. Pru Scott had only mentioned one person talking to her and that was a while before things got heavy.

Albie didn't get a chance to answer. A man came bounding up the courthouse steps towards them.

''Do you want to be on the telly?'' he asked.

''Who doesn't?'' said Albie.

*

The interview with Albie and Denny came up on the next day's edition of Six O'Clock Round Up which followed the early evening news. Albie went round to watch it with Denny at the flat. Tina was out shopping. She was still on holiday and enjoying every minute away from the reception desk of Planet Radio Repairs.

The television programme was introduced by cheery Terry James, or "Tel", as he was known to the viewing public. He was an ex-soccer-star-turned-TV-personality. The programme kicked off with a story about a woman who had been evicted from her council house because the loudness of her lovemaking kept the neighbours awake and was followed by the annual item warning people who bought puppies for Christmas presents not to chuck them out afterwards when they discovered how much it cost to feed them. Shots of barking mongrels in the cages of Battersea Dogs' Home. "Don't let your Christmas present end up here!"

Tel introduced all the items one after another with appropriate seriousness, indicated by the extent of forehead furrowing. All this time, Denny was tutting and swearing at the sheet of paper he was writing on.

"Something important, is it?" asked Albie.

"Yea," said Denny, "a poem."

Denny put his pen down when cheery Tel announced – with only medium forehead furrowing, thought Albie – the item on the inquest. It started off with some of the footage the television crew had shot of the courtroom exterior with Pope's voice on the soundtrack talking about the work of INCIDENT. Then came Denny and Albie.

"Despite this inquest we are still demanding a full scale public inquiry into the police action on that day," said Denny. "We find it incredible that a man can die in the streets of London without a criminal investigation being called."

114

Albie hadn't realised before seeing himself on the screen that Denny was just a bit taller than he was. He was also a bit put out to see that his hair looked grubby. "Yeah," he heard himself saying on the screen, "it's funny that someone can die in the middle of a crowd of coppers without there being one witness." Blimey, he sounded so common, too!

As the shot closed in on Albie, Denny realised that his contribution was over.

"Hey," he shouted at the screen. "They've cut out my bit about the class aspects of the inquest, haven't they?" He screwed a piece of paper into a ball and tossed it at the set. It bounced off the image of Albie's nose. "Bastards," he said.

One bit Albie was surprised they'd left in however came up next.

"And then another time I was forcibly taken to the local football ground," he was saying. "A bloke in a private box there was organising the giving out of right-wing leaflets. He told me that he wanted me on their side and to say things at the inquest which weren't true."

The report ended with a few words from Pope about the importance of keeping the police in check and then it was back to a deeply forehead-furrowed Tel. Behind Tel was a television set. He said: "Because of the magnitude of the allegations made by one of the people in the last report regarding right-wing political activities at one of England's top clubs we asked for a comment from the team's management. At very short notice, club director Ronnie Riley has kindly agreed to grant us an interview." Tel's fingers twiddled with an earphone. "And I think... do we?... yes, we can go over now to Ronnie Riley in our Manchester studios. He's there at a Football Association conference."

The television set behind Tel flickered and the smiling

face of a chubby, middle-aged man appeared on screen. He too was fumbling with an earphone.

"Hello, Ronnie."

"Hello, Tel."

"Tell me, Ronnie, what's all this about right-wing infiltration at your club's grounds?"

Ronnie chuckled. "Well, Tel, heaven above knows the truth behind it all but" – Ronnie looked serious – "you know as well as I do that a soccer crowd is a reflection of society. No doubt there are supporters of all political persuasions who attend our matches. We, off course, are opposed to the propagation of political propaganda of any kind at the ground itself. But you know as well as I do, Tel, that all sorts of things can happen in a large group of people that we can't check or have any jurisdiction over." He smiled resignedly.

Tel laughed. "Well, that's that out of the way," he said. "By the way, if your lads carry on performing as they have been over the past few matches you'll be a good bet for the League Cup later on in the season, eh, Ronnie?"

The chubby director returned to fiddling with his earphone. "Happy days are here again, Tel," said Ronnie Riley, or 'O', as he had been introduced to Albie at United's grounds.

Back to Tel. "Other news, just in, is that there has been another sighting of the famous Hackney Bear. A woman out walking her dog..."

Denny turned the television off.

Chapter 16

When Albie arrived for work the next morning there was an ambulance outside the back gates of Planet Radio Repairs. The gates were wide open. Two ambulance men scurried out and into the back of the revving vehicle, a fat roll of red blanket on the stretcher between them.

There had been an accident. It was obvious there had been an accident.

SLAM. The back doors of the ambulance SLAMMED. It was as if the doors had SLAMMED shut in the world's face. This was a private affair. With doors barely closed the ambulance moved off, purposefully but a little slow for Albie's liking, as if they knew it was too late.

Moving past the No Trespassing sign which clung on to the gate by a single nail, Albie moved into the uncovered yard. A couple of workers stamped their feet on the icy cobblestones. They stood hunchbacked, fags cupped in palms, and whispered to each other in short smoky bursts. A police constable appeared from inside the workshop entrance and told them they could go in now.

It was still early and there was hardly anyone else about in the workshop. Perhaps that was the reason it looked different. Another constable was inside, helmet off and notebook out. He was talking to Wilf the foreman who was sitting on a metal-topped work surface. Wilf looked childlike almost, his feet not quite touching the ground and the neat black shoes, as shiny as his hair, swinging back and forth to some inner, sorrowful, beat.

Albie looked round him. There was no sign of Denny yet. They had agreed to work this morning but they were going along to the afternoon session. Albie was to be called as a witness. It was the inquest's fourth day.

For some reason, Wilf looked calmer than Albie had ever seen him before, like a long AWOL squaddie relieved at his capture. He was chatting casually to the young constable who intermittently stabbed a pen sharply into his notebook.

"I was the first in this morning," said Wilf. "Well, *he* was first in, of course. I couldn't have been long after. He was always an early bird." He shook his head. "Not any more he won't be, not any more."

The other policeman asked the two workers who had just come in from the yard to help him raise the giant frame of the free-standing shelf unit back to its upright position. That was what had made the place look so different. The bloody thing had fallen over! The boxes and spare parts that had rested on its heavy metal shelves lay in a heap on the floor. In the middle of the chaos, however, was an ominous man-shaped clearing.

"Think I've found something here," the policeman called to his note taking partner as they stood the thing up. He was pointing towards the boot indented bottom shelf.

"Pinned to the floor like a bloody butterfly, he was," Wilf said dreamily. "Fixed by the wrists, knees, feet. His head must have smacked the concrete floor so hard..."

"It's easy to see how it happened," said the notetaker. "That unit wasn't connected to the wall properly, the lad must have been using that bottom shelf to reach up to the higher shelves."

Wilf nodded. "That's right. They've all been doing that because the step ladder's missing. Ray Ball took it home with him to do some home decorations. I knew some silly bugger would bring the whole thing down on top of themselves. I think I asked one of the lads to put it right.

118

But nobody takes any notice of what I say.'' Wilf swung his feet back and forth, back and forth.

Albie peered into the man-shaped hole. There was blood on the floor, a round, sticky, head-sized patch.

"I shifted the frame off the body single-handed," said Wilf, "but it didn't help. He was dead already." Wilf shook his head again. "He was all right, the lad was. Could be a right bolshie so and so but he was one of the best workers in the place."

The constable nodded sympathetically. "Doesn't particularly matter at the moment," he said, scribbling into the pad, "we can check it out later, but do you know if the lad's name really was Denny or was it short for Dennis?"

Albie reels out of Planet Radio Repairs. His head is a thin empty eggshell. He starts to laugh but he doesn't know why. Someone in the street says why are you laughing, man? Albie says I don't know why. A poster on the wall instructs him to buy a Zeta chocolate bar. He goes into a shop and picks up a Zeta chocolate bar but when the man behind the counter says where's your money he can't understand him, like he's talking another language. The man is talking another language. Albie laughs and drops the Zeta bar and he gets on a bus but he gets off the bus because it's going in the wrong direction. He gets on another bus and lights a fag. A woman says you can't smoke downstairs it's a disgusting habit and you should pack it up anyway. Albie says you're right and stubs the fag out and chucks the packet out of the window and never smokes again. He laughs and says it's bloody hot but someone says you're mad it's brass monkeys and Albie starts to shiver.

He gets off the bus and walks a bit. He rings on Denny and Tina's doorbell.

*

Directly above Albie's head, Tina threw open the top window and poked her head out.

"I'll be right down," she called out.

Albie was sure that he ought to be preparing what to say when the door opened but he couldn't think of anything that might possibly make it all easier. And he did so much want to make it all easier, as much for himself as for Tina.

It seemed an age before the door was pulled open. Tina stood inside looking a little dazed – in a cheery sort of way. She was wearing Denny's big Johnny "Duke" Andrews boxing gown and was puffing at the stub of a fat cigarette clenched between the points of an eyebrow tweezer.

She laughed: "Blimey, cheer up!"

Albie followed her in, through the damp hallway, watching all the way the outline of Tina's body as she stepped, a little unsteadily, upwards. Albie guessed that she was naked beneath the gown.

"I'll make some tea," said Tina as they entered the untidy flat. "I was halfway through the washing up when I thought how much more bearable it would be after a puff of this." She indicated the stub. "And now the washing up doesn't seem to matter anymore." She giggled.

Peering in through the kitchen door, Albie could see the huge sinkful of abandoned pots, pans and egg-stained breakfast plates. "I'll roll another one if you fancy a drag," she told Albie. Albie said he didn't.

"I'll roll one anyway," said Tina.

She put the kettle on and returned to Denny's little writing desk where she prepared the fat cigarette.

"I don't usually smoke at all during the daytime," she said apologetically, "but I feel so free, being away from Planet for a whole fortnight. I go back just before Christmas then I'll be off again almost immediately for the holidays."

The kettle whistled and she went to fetch two steaming

mugfuls of tea. She put the fat cigarette between her lips and lit up, sitting with her feet up on the sofa and puffing away merrily.

"It's really nice just having time off in London," said Tina. "I never was one for holidays in the sun. I went with Denny to Crete once. I felt like the bacon that gets left in the pan while you're paying the milkman." She took a sip of tea.

Albie opened his mouth to speak but Tina hadn't finished. "Have you ever noticed that there's one race that simply *everybody* hates – and that's the tourist race? The natives of the country they visit just about tolerate them as long as they're throwing money at them, but it's the other tourists who hate them." She giggled again. "You hear them moaning all the time when they get back to England, 'Oh, the place has got so *touristy*'. But what do they want? A shed in some one-horse town where they can't understand the lingo and the natives think they're loco?" She laughed out loud and took several more puffs, raising her leg so that the boxing gown parted to reveal her left thigh.

"But when you holiday in London," she went on, "you can do all the things you never get the chance to do when you're working. I've been to a few lunchtime theatre shows, seen a couple of films – the new Bob Hoskins one is good – done some shopping for clothes and spent a day in a posh sauna and…" Her voice trailed away and she smiled at Albie. "Come and sit down here, Albie," she said.

All the time, Albie had been standing stupidly with the cup of hot tea in his hand. He placed the cup on Denny's writing desk and crossed the room. Tina sat up to make room for him.

"You wouldn't believe some of the things I get up to on holidays, Albie," she said, giggling once again. "All those things you don't get a chance to do…" She let the unfinished sentence hang. She put her tea down and moved closer to Albie.

"I think there's something I should tell you," said Albie.

"Hush," she said, and put her fingers to his lips. "I know."

"You know?"

"I know you fancy me. That time here the other week. I didn't say no because I didn't fancy you too. It was just that the time wasn't right. It was all too sudden. And besides, Denny was expected home, wasn't he? But I mean, well, we're close friends, aren't we? It won't hurt just this once, will it? I think our relationship is strong enough to take it."

Tina stubbed the fat cigarette out in the ashtray and taking Albie's hand moved it between the folds of the boxing gown, just in case he hadn't got the message.

"Tina," said Albie, "there's something you ought to know."

"You're not going to tell me you've never tried it before, are you?" said Tina.

They went to the bedroom together.

Thinking about it afterwards, Albie couldn't believe that it had *really* happened like that, that he had been so blameless and passive, for in remembering that amorous struggle he recalled something other than love or even lust that had seeped out. He knew that even when he had discovered that Denny was the corpse they had carried out, something like this had been in his mind, a forbidden thing. There was aggression in his lovemaking, and selfishness, like this was something that was his by right. If the whole world could take advantage of him… well, wasn't it his turn?

He knew he would never forgive himself for that.

*

122

Albie sat upright at Denny's desk while Tina finished the washing up. He didn't know what he should be doing or saying. So he did nothing and said nothing. His now stone-cold cup of tea had pressed a circle into some writing on the notepad before him. It was a poem.

The poem was only a few lines long in rather difficult to read handwriting. He could just about make out the title. It said *For Tina*. Albie suddenly became aware that for some time Tina had been watching him. She smiled, drying her hands on a tea towel.

"Don't let Denny catch you reading that," said Tina. "He never lets me look at anything until he's fully satisfied with it. So I don't even dare peek. He says he's going to finish that one when he gets home tonight."

Chapter 17

Albie sat in the front row of the court gallery. He held on tight to the rail before him as if he were sitting in the front car of a fairground roller-coaster. The court went up and down and down and up as his head whirled. He so longed to have his feet planted once again on the ground. But that would have required a leap down to the hard surface below. And you can crack your head that way.

He had come directly from Tina to be at the afternoon session. He could still barely believe what had happened. Christ, he thought, looking round at the sea of blue uniformed police officers lining the walls of the room, if only they knew what partners we were. The coppers have killed one friend and I've killed another. And I've screwed his girlfriend before he was even fully cold.

Albie felt sick.

He tried to concentrate on the words of the witnesses. He couldn't imagine what he'd say when he was called. He was in no state at all.

Through the haze, Albie heard somebody called Casentino take the stand. Albie recalled that, like Parminder Haque, the man had come forward to say he saw Nicky getting hit by a policeman. Must concentrate, thought Albie, this is all about Nicky's death. But try as he might, his thoughts kept returning to Denny. He imagined that Tina had found out about his death by now. He pictured the look on her face. His head spun.

Mr Casentino took the stand.

Coroner Parkinson-Kettle looked up sharply and shuffled the papers about on his bench.

"Er, you are Mr Casentino, known as Mr Tasty-Lick, I understand," he said, hastily scanning one of the sheets in front of him.

Mr Casentino smiled. "That's right," he said, "I am Mr Tasty-Lick. To all the children I am Mr Tasty-Lick."

"Tell me Mr Casentino," said the coroner, "what is the nature of your occupation?"

Mr Casentino smiled patiently. "I'm an ice-cream man. I have a van. I was working in Circle Square on the day of the demonstration."

The coroner plucked his glasses from his face and ran his eye over Mr Casentino. "Would I be right in thinking," he asked, "that the ice-cream vending profession is one which has in the past been associated with various criminal elements?"

"I beg your pardon?" replied Mr Casentino, his smile visibly fading.

"Mr Casentino. I wonder if you could inform the court as to the nation of your origin."

Mr Casentino looked puzzled.

"Where do you come from?" bellowed Parkinson-Kettle.

"From Sicily."

"Sicily," said Parkinson-Kettle. "And would I be right in thinking that this is a part of the world famous for intense Mafia activity?"

Someone was calling Albie. Someone from a million miles away. Calling his name.

Albie was standing in the witness box. If asked, however, he wouldn't have been able to explain how he got there. He couldn't remember walking across the courtroom and

125

mounting the little wooden box. The whole room went up and down.

Albie held on to the edge of the stand for support.

Bringing the sea of faces before him into focus, Albie imagined that he was on a theatre stage and that the coroner, jury and press were his audience. But what was expected of him? He racked his brains for something he could do. He couldn't juggle, sing or tap dance. He couldn't play the accordion or pull a rabbit out of a hat. So what could he do?

But then all was made clear to him as Bow Tie Bradley started to speak. He was part of a double act of course; he was the stooge.

"Tell me," asked Bradley, smiling sympathetically, "how long had you and Nicky Turner known each other?"

"Oh, a good few years," Albie replied.

"A good few years," Bradley repeated to the jury as if a translation was required. "You had attended football matches together since your early teens, had you not?"

Albie's mind was wandering. "Sorry," he said. "Had we not what?"

"Attended football matches," said Bradley with impatience and raising his voice as if talking to a hard of hearing pensioner.

"Oh, but we did," said Albie. There were a few chuckles from the back of the court. Why, this stupid boy couldn't even understand the questions properly, Albie imagined them thinking. He explained that they'd played together in the Whitechapel Wanderers and also went to all of United's home fixtures. Bradley asked if they'd ever been involved in any trouble. Once or twice, Albie told him.

Among the faces, Albie could see Pope visibly pale.

"Would you describe Nicky Turner as somebody who could look after himself, Albie?" asked Bradley.

"Yes, I think so."

Bradley placed a single finger to his temple as if he were attempting to work out a complicated mathematical problem in his head. As far as Albie could make out though there was no logical progression from his last question to the next.

"Tell me, Albie, had Nicky Turner to your knowledge any political axe to grind? Was he dedicated to any particular causes that you knew of?"

The courtroom was spinning faster than ever. The double act of Bradley and Brownslow was dying on its feet. Albie just couldn't remember the punchlines.

"No, no," he heard himself saying. "Nicky was just one of the lads. All he was interested in was a few beers on Saturday night, doing a bit of chatting up and all the rest."

"What does 'all the rest' include, Albie?" wheedled the man in the bow tie. "Would it include the odd punch-up?"

Pope leapt to his feet to appeal to the coroner. Parkinson-Kettle wasn't having any of it, though. He shushed Pope and told Bradley to continue. Albie was still shaking his head.

"No, no," he said, "Nicky wasn't one to go looking for trouble."

"And yet you have told the court that Nicky Turner was quite capable of 'looking after himself'. You must have seen him involved in situations of conflict to know that."

Albie shook his head up and down and from side to side. He shrugged his shoulders. Parkinson-Kettle intervened, telling Albie he had to speak aloud.

"Yea, well, I suppose so," he said quietly. Bradley's blue eyes sparkled. Pope put his head in his hands.

"Albie Brownslow," asked Bradley, "would you explain the reason behind your own and Nicky Turner's presence on that march?"

But Albie couldn't answer. He felt sick. Everybody was looking towards him awaiting the finale – but his throat had dried up and he couldn't move his feet.

Albie imagined he saw Tina appear in a puff of smoke at the back of the court and Bradley's bow tie start to spin round and round, bright red sparks flying off it like a firework. "Why did you go on the march? Why did you go on the march?" he was shouting.

He never got an answer. The whole court stared at Albie as he crumpled like a reverse jack-in-the-box, his head causing a loud crack to echo round the room as it made contact with the wooden floor.

Chapter 18

The next morning, Albie's mum said he shouldn't go to the inquest. He couldn't be well, fainting like that. Albie said he'd be all right. He got to the court right at the last minute as people were being ushered in. Pope looked pale and shaken. Wasn't it terrible about Denny's death? Yes, it was. Did Albie know how it had happened? Yes, he did. Did he know who was responsible? No, he couldn't imagine.

Coroner Parkinson-Kettle told the jury that he was now going to ask them to consider the medical evidence surrounding the events of November 5th. He was going to call the two pathologists who had examined the body.

Professor Nelson had been the first person to examine the body. He was a tall, square-headed man with a clipped moustache and grey hair. The coroner pushed his glasses up high on his nose and sat forward in his chair as the professor nodded politely in the direction of the jury. When he spoke it was with an unexpected Yorkshire accent. He explained at length details of the dates and times when he had examined the body and how he had come to the conclusion that Nicky's death had resulted from a single blow to the left side of the head. There were no other injuries. Professor Nelson said that he had discovered Nicky's skull to be abnormally thin and that the same pressure inflicted on somebody with an average skull thickness almost certainly wouldn't have resulted in death. He went on: ''The surprising feature is the tremendous bone damage caused without external damage to the skin. This would, in fact, exclude a police truncheon as a possible weapon." The coroner smiled. Professor Nelson continued: "A police truncheon is relatively light, you see? And usually lacerates the scalp."

Parkinson-Kettle asked the professor if he had seen the display of equipment the police had taken out with them that day. He had. And was there anything there that could have caused the blow? "Yes," said the professor. "A police radio."

The coroner thanked the professor profusely, with much smiling and gesturing for him to step down from the stand. He said he was going to take the evidence of the other pathologist before he'd allow questions from the two solicitors.

With the money raised by the sale of posters and collections at meetings, INCIDENT had commissioned an independent autopsy on Nicky's body. Albie figured they couldn't have had much to spend because what they got was Professor Byron, a small elderly man with a limp. When he spoke it was with a thin, dry voice. He seemed to know his stuff well enough, though.

There didn't seem to be any argument at all between the two professors about the cause of Nicky's death, but Byron said that although Nicky's skull was a little on the thin side he wouldn't have described it as abnormally thin. Good gracious no. He also said that in his opinion the blow must have been very severe indeed. "A deliberate blow from a hand-held object, a swinging blow from one side."

The coroner looked upset. He removed his glasses to give them a rub. "As for the police radio theory," continued Byron with his eyebrows raised, "it is very unlikely indeed that it could have been the weapon. It is after all a comparatively flimsy object. I should imagine it could produce an injury if an officer were to swing it round and round his head by the aerial." There was some laughter from the public gallery. Coroner Parkinson-Kettle raised an admonishing eyebrow.

There was no stopping Byron now that he'd started. "No, no, certainly not a radio," he continued, raising a hand to his chin, "I'd say the blow would more likely have been caused by something like a blackjack."

"The coroner gasped. "A blackjack!" he exclaimed, interrupting the Professor. "And are the police equipped with such weaponry?"

"Not that I know of," said Byron.

"Not that you know of," said the coroner, speaking slowly, pronouncing each word separately and clearly as if the professor had given himself away in some way.

"Not officially," added Byron.

It was all too much for Parkinson-Kettle. "Is not a blackjack more likely to be the sort of weapon which would be taken on a demonstration by a troublemaker?" he bellowed across the courtroom.

"None were found on those arrested as I understand," said Byron.

"Thank you, Professor Byron," said the coroner, slamming his spectacles back on his nose.

They adjourned for lunch.

During the break, the photographer Elliott Ness came bounding into the courthouse entrance hall. It must have been snowing outside again because he was beating snowflakes from his woolly hat.

He approached Pope and they had a whispered conversation, Pope slowly nodding his head up and down.

After lunch, the two professors were brought back to the witness stand.

"Was there any possibility that Nicholas Turner was hit by a cricket bat?" asked the coroner. The expert opinion from both professors was that there was no possibility of this at all.

"Er, why do you ask?" ventured Professor Byron.

"There was a cricket bat found amongst the objects taken from the demonstrators," the coroner explained.

It was then time for the solicitors' questions. Pope, once again a model of composure, was on first. Nelson was in the witness box.

"Professor Nelson," began Pope, pulling his pipe from his pocket, "when you examined the body of this fit and agile young man, did it immediately enter your head that he had met his death through a single blow from such a lightweight item as a police radio?"

"No, of course not," said the large Yorkshireman, shuffling his feet slightly. "But taking into consideration the possible objects which I have seen..."

Pope was quick off the mark. He moved towards the grey-haired man. "So, in fact, you're telling us, are you not, Professor Nelson, that of the weapons you have been shown a police radio is the most likely to have caused the injury?"

Nelson had to concede that.

"Professor Nelson," continued Pope, tapping his chin with the stem of his unlit pipe, "as a pathologist, is it not your duty to come to your own conclusions about the nature of the weapon used, rather than to take your pick from a selection presented to you by the police?"

But Nelson did not get a chance to answer.

Coroner Parkinson-Kettle intervened: "It should be pointed out, Mr Pope, that at an inquest you examine witnesses, you do not cross-examine them. You are not allowed to attempt to discredit witnesses. You may only ask questions relevant to how, when and where the deceased died."

Next, it was Bow-Tie Bradley's turn with Byron. He smiled in the direction of the jury. Albie even imagined he saw him tip the merest hint of a wink at the woman in the furry boots.

132

"Pathology is not an exact science," said Bradley, accusingly.

"No," Professor Byron agreed.

"You sometimes have to indulge in speculation and guesswork?"

"I try not to but, yes, sometimes it is necessary."

"There is no evidence that the police went to the demonstration armed with blackjacks, like some sordid gang of the Victorian underworld, is there?"

"No."

"But they were equipped with radios. And, as we have heard from an expert, a blow from a radio could have caused the injury, perhaps accidentally..."

"Well..."

"It's a perfectly good possibility. Why are you so grudging about it?"

"I cannot exclude the possibility entirely," was all Byron would say. Bradley seemed happy with that and the coroner called it a day.

As they were shuffling out of the courtroom, Pope told Albie that there had been some developments concerning the photographs. He was going round to see Elliott Ness later and he suggested that Albie meet him there.

Elliott Ness lived in a mews flat off Kingsland High Road in Dalston.

The walls of the hallway were covered with photographs including some fashion shots. "Friends of mine who come here say, why have you got them up there, man," said Ness, "but I reckon there's no one you can't learn from, right? The first time I went to *City Lights* was to do some photos for a feature on women's tights. They assumed I was the guy they'd hired to do a photo essay on Brixton. I've never looked back since."

Pope had arrived a little before Albie. He was just fixing himself a cup of coffee and was searching for sugar on a cluttered work surface as Albie and Ness entered the room. Ness showed them enlargements of the Circle Square photographs. They were the same shots they had seen before, but blown up to poster size, all sorts of minor details were apparent.

"It's weird," said Ness. "I didn't really see half these things myself when I was taking the pictures. It's like when I got back from St Lucia the other summer. People asked me what it was like and I told them that I wouldn't know until I got my films developed. But even when I do see something," Ness went on, "even something like Nicky Turner's death, I don't feel anything. No anger, hatred, fear, danger, injustice or the urge to get stuck in there. Nothing. All part of the photographer's job to remain the impartial observer, I suppose." He shrugged.

Elliott Ness said that he had been in contact with Tina since they had met at Pope's place and that he had been round to console her over Denny's death. "She's taking it real hard," he said.

"I can imagine," said Albie.

"You've not been round yourself to see her yet then?" asked Pope, diverting his gaze towards Albie temporarily.

Albie looked to the floor. "I just don't know what I'd say to her," he mumbled. "I've thought of nothing else since it happened. I keep imagining the accident over and over as if it'll come out different one time and Denny won't be dead after all."

There was an awkward silence which Elliott Ness tried to fill. "The police start to give evidence tomorrow," he said. "Reckon there's any chance of us recognising the copper in these pictures?"

"That copper won't even be there," said Pope. "He's bound to be one of the three they're pretending wasn't

134

there. But I'll get on to Starling and find out if there's any way we can get a good look at them."

There was another pause as they gazed deep into the part of the policeman's face which was visible in one of the photographs.

"Notice anything about his mouth?" said Ness. They all nodded. The man's mouth was partially open. It could be seen that there was a gap in the otherwise clear row of teeth, as though the tooth wasn't there.

Albie found the next day of the inquest the most depressing since Nicky died. One by one, the Unit 3 SPG officers took the stand to answer questions from Bow-Tie Bradley and Pope, although in Bradley's case they were merely asked to affirm his assumption that they were wonderful, responsible, nice young lads. Pope's questions were treated with contempt.

"PC Hayter," asked Pope, "why were your truncheons drawn when you charged the demonstrators?"

PC Hayter grinned at the stupidity of the question. "We were under attack, sir. We were in the middle of the worst anti-police riot I had ever seen. People were lobbing rocks and milk bottles at us. Inspector Walker got hit on the shoulder by something as we got out the van."

"Will you please tell the court how many people were arrested for throwing missiles at the police?" asked Pope.

The officer looked skywards as if making a calculation. "None," he said finally. There was laughter from the other police in the court.

"That's presumably because not one could be identified?"

"I'd say that's correct, sir. When you're confronted by a massive crowd it's difficult to pick out individuals."

"So you would agree that it would be totally unjustifiable to hit out at an individual when nobody could definitely be identified as a stonethrower?''

"Er, I think that's what I might mean, sir, perhaps."

"Is it not the case then, PC Hayter, that Nicky Turner was attacked as a random retribution for the half brick that hit Inspector Walker on the shoulder, and that he was hit as he was running away from the police as witnesses have stated?''

PC Hayter looked from side to side in an exasperated manner as if he were being asked for money by a dosser who had him by the lapels, rather than being questioned about the facts surrounding a murder. "Let's face it sir,'' he said angrily, "there weren't any non-biased bystanders around at the time the police charged. I mean, all the witnesses were taking part in the demonstration or they were foreigners. I mean, they're bound to have a grudge, aren't they?''

Pope made mouths like a goldfish and looked towards the coroner. Parkinson-Kettle said nothing. He took off his glasses when he noticed Pope looking at him.

PC Baylis was next. Apart from Inspector Walker, he had been the oldest officer in the vans. Even so, he didn't look much over thirty.

"PC Baylis,'' asked Pope, "is it ever necessary in your opinion for a policeman to hit a member of the public?''

"I think it is, sir. Yes, I know it is.''

"Was the incident in Circle Square one where it was necessary for policemen to hit people?''

Baylis was wary of traps. "Perhaps not, sir,'' he said.

Pope looked genuinely taken aback. "No?'' he said. "Even though you claim that there was a riot going on?''

"That's right, sir.''

"And yet some policemen did hit people, didn't they? The local hospital was full of demonstrators with head injuries. Nicky Turner died of just such an injury.''

"I didn't see anybody hitting anybody, sir."

Pope exploded. "What, even though you were all running with your truncheons drawn? You a policeman, trained to observe details and violent actions, did not see anybody hit out or being hit?"

"I was too busy trying to disperse the crowd, sir."

"PC Baylis," said Pope, "what you are in fact telling us is that if anybody was hit by a police truncheon it would be by your own admission a wholly unnecessary and possibly illegal action?"

"I can't speak for other officers who might have interpreted the situation differently, sir."

"PC Baylis, if I am correct, you are telling the court that there was no reason to hit anybody, so therefore no policeman would have done such a thing, but if a policeman had hit somebody then of course it must have been necessary – but you didn't see anything anyway."

PC Baylis smirked. "That about sums it up, sir."

During the lunch break, Pope seemed to be in a curious state of anger and glee. Despite the bad morning he was sure of some big revelations in the afternoon. The very next police witness due up was one of those who, according to Starling, had not been on the original list.

Pope had his pipe at the ready as the jury reassembled. The woman in the furry boots had obviously been out for lunch because a light fall of snow was visible on her head and shoulders. Pope was tapping his pipe stem thoughtfully on his chin as PC Velos mounted the witness stand. He was obviously eager to get stuck in.

"Is it the case, PC Velos, that all SPG vans are required to keep a log of officers on board?"

"That's correct, sir," said the young officer.

"Could you describe this to the court?"

"Yes, it's a loose-leaf file with a page for each day."

"So it's not impossible that a page could be removed and

replaced with another sheet?''

"I don't know what you're getting at, sir."

"Don't you, PC Velos? What if I were to suggest to you that your name did not appear on the original sheet for that day?"

Parkinson-Kettle's face started to redden.

"I would further suggest," said Pope, "that your name didn't appear on the list because you never were in the van on that day and that your name replaced that of another officer who was."

Parkinson-Kettle shouted across the courtroom: "Mr Pope! I would ask you to remember that you are not allowed to cross-examine the witnesses. Your suggestions are totally out of order and as far as I can see without foundation. I would ask the jury to disregard your comments and have them struck from the records. If you broach this subject again I shall declare you in contempt of court."

The two men stared at each other, Pope sucking the air in through his pipe and exhaling it through clenched teeth.

There was worse to come. At the end of the day Parkinson-Kettle removed his glasses, sniffed and dabbed his nose with his hankie. "There have been two extreme theories mooted in this court about Nicholas Turner's death that I consider without foundation," he said. "One theory is that one of the demonstrators killed him in the hope of suspicion being thrown on the police and therefore creating a martyr. The other extreme theory is that he was killed by a policeman wielding an unauthorised weapon."

Pope looked horrified. "Forgive me," he called out, interrupting the coroner. "I don't know where on earth you got your first 'extreme theory' from but it's not one that's been heard in this court. To lump it together with the second theory for which there *is* evidence is to try to dismiss them both.''

Stephen ''Bow Tie'' Bradley looked as if butter wouldn't melt in his mouth. His lip curled into a smile as he allowed himself another glance in the direction of the fur-booted female juror.

Parkinson-Kettle was speechless. He started to bang the little gavel by his hand on the desk for the first time in the proceedings – just like a real judge.

But Pope wouldn't shut up. As he waved his pipe in the air while haranguing the coroner it occurred to Albie that it had remained unlit all day. And in thinking about it he realised that in all the times he'd seen Pope with his pipe he could never remember him puffing smoke through it. Quite simply, Pope didn't smoke.

Chapter 19

It was Saturday morning. The first week of the inquest was over.

Albie and Simon Pope stood across the street from the Central London police station watching the entrance. Detective Sergeant Starling had informed them that PC Green – one of the three "vanishing" policemen whose names had been removed from the police log – was based there.

Starling had given them the number of Green's car so they simply waited until he came out and got into it. The snow was hard and crunchy under their feet as they approached the vehicle. Albie pulled the collar of his raincoat up, imagining himself to be some sort of Humphrey Bogart. Pope did all the talking. He pulled his pipe from his mouth with a woolly-gloved hand.

"Excuse me, PC Green," said Pope, tapping on the window. The policeman wound the window down, suspicion heavy on his thickset features. He must have been wondering how Pope knew his identity.

"What are you, an autograph hunter?" said the policeman.

"I'd like to have it at the bottom of a statement," replied Pope.

PC Green bared his teeth. He seemed to have the full set. "If you're going to muck about, pal..."

"Try this out," said Pope, crouching down and raising his pipe to his lips, "on November 5th this year, you and two of your buddies were on duty at a demonstration in the Unit 3 SPG van which entered Circle Square. And yet when we look at the log for the day we find your name isn't there.''

"Funny, eh?'' said PC Green.

"Somebody falsified that log after the event when it was discovered that one of you three had killed Nicky Turner.''

"I think you must have had too much to drink at the office party, pal,'' said the policeman, starting to wind the car window up.

"We have it from a reliable source that our information is correct.''

The policeman stopped winding the window up and smiled wearily. "And very useful your source is going to be if he doesn't come out into the open, isn't he?'' he said.

Pope continued: "The coroner isn't planning to finish his summing up until early next week – on Christmas Eve. There's still time for new evidence to be submitted. What makes you think our bird won't sing?''

"Self-preservation, that's what. Your source must be a copper, right? Squealers in the Force never see promotion. They quite often leave altogether because of the bad feeling. And what is there outside the force for ex-coppers? They all end up as supermarket security men. Your source most likely just has a grudge.''

Pope waved his pipe – unlit as always – about him. "And what motives can there be for the cynical deception you are attempting?''

"Loyalty,'' said the policeman, unhesitatingly.

"Loyalty,'' repeated Pope. "Is that justification for abuse of power?''

"Loyalty is justification for anything. Loyalty to family, friends, a cause, a movement. People don't live by the ten commandments, you know. All God need have written on those tablets of stone was one word – loyalty.''

PC Green went to wind the window up but Pope thrust his woolly-gloved hand in to hold it open. This angered the policeman inside. "Your source," he shouted, "won't go public because he wants to stay in the Force. That's because he thinks he's doing a good job keeping an eye on all us bastards. And perhaps he is. You can be as saintly as you like in the Force, but it's us sinners who get the results. Fire with fire. We spar with the devil so we can win on points when the big fight comes up." He started to rev the engine up.

"Look," shouted Pope through the gap, "I came here to offer you a deal. I know that you're one of the three officers whose names were removed from the log book. One of you killed Nicky Turner and the other two know it. That's why your names were replaced. If you denounce one of the others as the killer you'll only be disciplined. Otherwise you could face a charge of murder."

The policeman raised his eyebrows. "But what if it was me who killed the Turner lad?"

"Look," said Pope, "at this stage in the proceedings I'm just looking for a result."

PC Green burst out laughing. "So, that's what this pathetic little attempt at blackmail is all about," he said, "the furtherance of your reputation as a champion for the downtrodden."

"Justice must be seen to be done," said Pope.

PC Green shoved the car into gear and it started to move off. "Oh, that'll happen all right," he said. "Justice will be *seen* to be done – even if it isn't being done."

Pope had to wrench his hand away from the car window as the vehicle disappeared in a cloud of exhaust smoke. Pope's glove went with it.

"Damn it," said Pope, wringing his bruised, bare hand in the cold air. "This sort of confrontation isn't going to get us anywhere." He looked embarrassed and angry. He started to stomp off in the hard snow. He didn't look at Albie as he spoke. "You have a go at tracking down the

142

other two vanishing policemen tomorrow. See what they look like. Can't do any harm. I'll get Starling to give you a call on their whereabouts. We also need some provable link between the killer and whoever changed that log book entry."

For some reason, Albie had never told Pope, Denny or anybody else in INCIDENT about the suspicions he had that the person who'd tampered with the records was Cobb. He didn't know why really. But then perhaps he did.

On Sunday morning Starling telephoned Albie at home. He said: "Do you know the Hammersmith area at all, Albie?"

Albie said he didn't.

"Under the flyover, right outside the Hammersmith Odeon. One-thirty this afternoon. Tell me, Albie, what's red outside, white inside and sings the *Horst Wessel Lied*?" Starling hung up.

The answer was a red Sierra with PC Currie – the second "vanishing policeman" – and O and Ginger inside. Albie watched from the Odeon entrance as Ginger stepped out of the stationary vehicle. As PC Currie and O chatted it was just possible to make out that Currie had all his teeth but impossible to imagine what he and O might be saying to each other in the front seats. Albie followed Ginger who was walking dejectedly round the corner.

Ginger wandered along a row of shops looking in the windows, her big black Doc Martens pounding holes in the snow. She finally entered a Pie & Mash shop. It had a traditional Edwardian frontage and, just inside, a bespectacled man with an axe could be seen pulling live eels out of a bucket and chopping them into thick, wriggling chunks.

Ginger took a plateful of food from the counter and sat herself down at one of the heavy, marble-topped tables. Albie went in and sat opposite her. "Mind if I sit and watch you eat?" he asked.

Ginger was very good at not looking surprised. "My mum always told me never to speak to strange men," she said, barely raising her eyes from the full plate.

"Really?" said Albie. "You seem to have been making a lot of strange friends lately."

"You and me both, eh?" said Ginger, slicing through the flaky pastry topping to the heart of the pie.

"You don't think it's a coincidence that I saw you getting booted out of that car, do you?"

Ginger made eye-contact with Albie at last. "How did you know we'd be here?" she said.

"A little bird told me."

Ginger speared a piece of eel on her fork and pushed it around in the thick green parsley sauce before putting it in her mouth.

"So what's the summit meeting about?" asked Albie.

Ginger laughed. "They're discussing the team's chances for the European cup next year."

"It's OK," said Albie. "I don't expect you to tell me because you don't know. They turfed you out of the car so the grown-ups could talk."

Ginger actually looked hurt. Her jaw stopped chewing. "Well, I do know, so there," she said. "After you opened your big mouth on that television programme, O's worried there might be an F.A. investigation into what's going on at the United football grounds. He's telling PC Currie now that if that happens he's going to make trouble for the police."

"But what's O got on the police?" questioned Albie. He shook his head. "There's something missing, Ginger, and whatever it is must relate to the march – except that O's

144

mob weren't even there."

"I don't know," said Ginger. "I trust O in all his actions. I don't care about what happened on the march."

"Ginger," said Albie, "it's your brother you're talking about. It was your brother Nicky who died."

"Listen, Albie," said Ginger, stirring the sauce into the lumpy mashed potatoes, "I'm not against the police smashing lefties' skulls in but they didn't get a lefty, they got Nicky. And I blame your lot for that."

Albie shook his head. "Why have you become a part of all this, Ginger?" he said. "Let's face it, you're a foot-soldier like me. The generals sitting and plotting in the car round the corner don't give a toss about you. Why do you want to win their respect so much when in fact they despise your sort? *Our* sort!"

Ginger slammed her knife and fork down on the half full plate loudly, so that everyone else in the place turned round to look at her. "Don't you talk about *our* sort," she spat. "It's *your* sort who've presided over the mongrel-isation of our British race."

"Bugger race," said Albie, "it's class that matters, and class is wider than nationality. You and me, Ginger, we're working class. The media, the law, the likes of O – they're all just taking us for a ride."

Ginger faked a yawn, which, as she had a mouthful of food, wasn't a pretty sight.

"I'll tell you something else you don't know," continued Albie. "PC Currie – the copper in the car with O – is one of those we think killed Nicky. Funny how they didn't let you in on that one, isn't it?"

Ginger picked up the remains of the food and with what Albie thought was an uncharacteristic subtle wrist move-ment, propelled the plate so that it slapped straight on to Albie's chest. Pie, mash, eel and sauce ran down his white shirt. He moved forward sharply, trying to prevent as much of it as possible from falling into his lap. The axeman at the window paused in his executions to see what was going on. He raised a bloodied hand to push his glasses up on his nose. Ginger stood up.

"You tell lies and O tells the truth. It's as simple as that," she shouted, walking to the shop doorway. "Nicky was everything to me," she said, "a friend as well as a brother. I believed in him but now he doesn't exist anymore. Now I believe in O. You wait, he's gonna get you, he is." She left the shop.

Albie followed her to the door and shouted after her: "Screw O – he's nothing but a big fat zero."

There was a car outside the Pie & Mash shop with a man sitting at the wheel. It took a couple of seconds before Albie recognised him. It was the dapper Commander Powell. The curious thing was that when he looked across and saw Albie standing there – eel and pie dripping off his chest – he immediately put down the radio handset he was holding and started up the car. He didn't acknowledge Albie but sped off, leaving Albie to ponder what it all meant.

Waiting for the bus, it occurred to Albie that all the time they had been talking, Ginger had been pitching her comments on the assumption that Albie was a lefty. And thinking about it, Albie supposed that he was.

That same evening, Albie set off on the trail of PC Rivers, the third "vanishing" policeman. He had a copy of that day's *Sunday Telegraph* – nice and big – to hold up in front of his face in case PC Rivers looked in his direction. Also, in his pocket he had sufficient cash – he hoped – in case he had to jump in a cab and yell "Follow that car". Yes, he was quite looking forward to that.

As it happened though, when PC Rivers emerged from

the Central London police station wearing a light raincoat, he jumped straight on to a bus. He was easily recognisable from the description Starling had given Albie on the telephone. He was tall and blond with a fairly fresh scar down one side of his face. Albie was familiar with the number 15 bus route, in fact it passed close to where he lived. Rivers sat upstairs right at the front. Albie sat at the back, the newspaper poised at the ready in case he needed it to mask his face.

When the conductor came to collect Albie's fare it must have been obvious that he didn't know where he was going. Albie dropped a few coins into the man's hand. "As far as you go," he mumbled.

The bus ploughed through the city and straight back into the shabby East End which Albie had left just a few hours earlier. Where could Rivers be going?

When the policeman finally got up Albie sat with the newspaper on his lap staring straight ahead of him hoping that Rivers wouldn't recognise him. As it was, the police-man didn't even notice him. He was peering out through the window, obviously not at all sure where he was.

He got off the bus at the stop in Commercial Road that Albie always got off at when he took this bus.

Albie kept his distance, noting that every now and then Rivers would pull a small book from his pocket, already folded back from the spine at a central page. Albie deduced it must have been an A-Z streetmap because Rivers would look down into it and up to the street signs before tucking it away again in his raincoat pocket. The policeman seemed to be heading straight towards Albie's tower block.

At the base of the block, the policeman paused to look up. Albie trailed along behind, not really trying to hide any more as he watched Rivers press the button and wait for the lift.

Albie took the stairs. Letting himself into the flat, he could hear voices. He recognised those of Mum, Cobb and Shirley Bassey. There was one other. In the living room, Cobb was opening a bottle of wine while Mum was bringing in a couple of bowls of peanuts and Twiglets from the kitchen.

"Albie," called Cobb, a little flustered, "wasn't expecting you in tonight. Meet my brother-in-law. Brother-in-law in more ways than one, if you see what I mean?" Cobb waved his hand in the direction of PC Rivers who opened his mouth in the shape of a smile. One tooth was much darker than the rest, like it wasn't there.

Chapter 20

Monday, the day before Christmas Eve. First thing in the morning, Albie bounded up the stairs of Planet Radio Repairs and straight into the reception area. Two young men in suits were sitting together in the low comfy chairs opposite Tina's desk. They were slowly turning over the pages of a glossy, leatherbound folder which they had placed on the glass-topped coffee table between them.

"If we really hammer home the success of our Hewitt's Ale beer mat campaign I reckon that'll swing it for us," said one to the other, dabbing a finger on to the page open before them.

Tina was sitting behind her desk, her head turned away. Albie leaned over towards her in a confidential manner.

"Tina," he whispered, "I've found out one or two things that could stand the inquest on its head. All along I've been pretty sure that it was Cobb who got the Unit 3 log changed. Now we've got a provable link..." He stopped there, for as she turned towards him, Albie could see that Tina had been crying. She had no make-up on for once and looked pale, as if she hadn't slept for a couple of nights. She stared directly into Albie's eyes and he automatically took a step backwards.

"We should also point out the proven seven and a half per cent increase in the sales of Bigelow Crisps during just their first six months with our agency," said a voice behind Albie.

"Yes," said Tina in a low voice. "I found out."

Albie wanted to say something, not really knowing what he'd say even if he had a chance to say it.

149

"I didn't find out about Denny until that afternoon, Albie. A copper came round to tell me. How do you think I felt after we'd spent the morning together, Albie?" Tina screwed her eyes up. "How do you think I felt?"

Albie wanted to say something – but again, not really.

"And how do you think I bloody well felt when I found out that you already knew about Denny?"

The two men in suits stopped talking. "*Language*," one said to the other in mock shock but not really mock shock.

"She looks such a decent girl too," the other said jokingly and not at all jokingly.

"I think your despicable," said Tina, her voice steadily rising. "I can't believe what happened. We were friends, Albie, working together to discover the truth about what happened in Circle Square, and you haven't even been in touch since Denny died." Tina was shouting now. "You must frighten yourself, Albie. You're hollow. You have no morals, no principles, you're a vacuum waiting for something, anything, to fill it and you don't care what."

"What's she on about?" said one of the men in suits.

"Don't know, vacuum cleaners or something," said the other.

"Tina," blurted Albie, searching for a cliché, "I can explain everything."

"Everything," yelled Tina, "amounts to this: you found out that my boyfriend – your friend – was dead. So the first thing that occurred to you was to come round and give me a poke. That's what happened."

The loud bangs behind him were probably the young men's jaws hitting the floor, thought Albie. It wasn't, though, it was Ball opening and shutting the door to his office. He'd obviously heard the whole conversation. He stormed up to the reception desk, pulsing with rage. Even at this early hour he brought the smell of alcohol with him.

"Shut up, shut up, you two," he shouted, casting a

sideways glance in the direction of the two young ad-men. "You're both sacked. I've never heard such foul language in all my life. And in a reception area as well." Ball said the words "reception area" in the same sort of tone that a vicar might say "place of worship".

"As for you, Tina," Ball said, trying to calm himself a little, "if I'd known that you were living with – well, not to speak ill of the dead – but if I'd known that you and Denny were mixed up in this Circle Square business you'd have both been out on your ears long ago. I'll not be ungenerous at this time, though. I'll give you a couple of months' money and that's the end of it, all right?"

Tina got up and yanked the top drawer of her desk open wide. "You can stuff your money," she said, throwing make-up, pens and pencils into her fat handbag. "I'm going to finish off the work that Denny started on the Turner inquest. Somebody's got to see it through and it's obvious that nobody round here really cares about who dies as long as they can screw people – one way or the other. I don't actually want to spend the rest of my life with crooks and con men, wide boys, liars and opportunists. I'm funny like that." She smiled curtly at Albie and Ray Ball, closed up her bag, put on her coat and walked out of the door. Albie and Ball stood side by side, confused at being cast as allies. Behind them, one of the young men coughed politely. "If it were more convenient for you, Mr Ball, we could always, you know, call back another, you know, more convenient…"

Albie flattened out a ball of paper left on Tina's desk. It turned out to be the sheet with Denny's final poem on it: *For Tina*.

Chapter 21

Cobb was standing in the hallway when Albie arrived home. He stood boldly but open-mouthed as he had when Albie had discovered him on the night Mum had announced their marriage. He wasn't naked and carrying teas, though. He was fat with fur coat and shoulder bags and carrying two leather suitcases, brand new by the look of them. One still had a price tag on it. Cobb either hadn't shaved for a few days or was growing a beard. On his head was one of those furry Russian hats, far too big for him. It came right down over his ears and the back of his neck so that he resembled a Laurel & Hardy film interpretation of a Klondike gold digger.

"Where are you going?" asked Albie.

"Me and your mother, we're off on our delayed honeymoon," said Cobb. "We told you about it, remember."

No, Albie didn't remember. He certainly hadn't expected Mum to steal away just before Christmas.

Albie moved past Cobb, looking in all the rooms of the flat. "Where's Mum now, then?" he asked. Cobb looked dreadful in the glare of the low hall light which dangled just inches above his furry head. His skin behind the untidy stubble looked like cold tapioca pudding, a couple of deeply imbedded prunes for eyes.

"My wife is already at the airport," Cobb told him, aggression returning to his voice. "I told her to go ahead and get a standby flight fixed up. I've been working right up to the last minute, see? It's Christmas Eve tomorrow, Albie. If we don't get away now we never will. See you in a fortnight." He turned to go.

"By which time the inquest and media interest in it will be over, right?"

Cobb looked over his shoulder. "You what?"

"Tomorrow's the last day of the inquest, Inspector Cobb. I want you to go there and tell them that you know it was PC Rivers, your brother-in-law, who killed Nicky, and that you changed the log to make it look like he wasn't on duty at the demo."

Cobb shrugged and put on a "who me?" expression.

"I realised later on," continued Albie, "that you came here the morning after the murder to find out what I had seen. I was going to tell INCIDENT about all my suspicions until you and Mum started to... well, started. And then I thought about how it might all affect her."

Cobb started to walk the length of the hall towards the front door.

"Inspector Cobb," called Albie, "you can't just turn your back on this."

Cobb looked back, and bending at the knees, rested the suitcases on the floor. "You can't bring back the dead," he said simply.

"You're doing wrong," said Albie. "Don't you see that? It's time you investigated yourself, Cobb. The investigation never stops. You told me that."

"This particular case is closed, Albie. The investigation into the meaning of life is wider than just one death. The nature of the investigation changes, sometimes it switches to different locations. In my case it's switching to a fortnight in Florida with your mum. Just think, for her it's the chance of a lifetime. Something she's never been able to afford before. I'll send you a postcard. Bye." He turned to go.

As Cobb picked up the cases, Albie moved quickly into his bedroom. Cobb had the front door open as Albie re-emerged into the hallway clutching Nicky's pellet-gun.

At this point, people in films say things like: "Well, I'm afraid with what you know I'm not going to be able to let you leave." So that's what Albie said.

Cobb, hearing a threat in Albie's voice, slowly turned round, once again lowering the suitcases to the floor. "What's that you've got there, Albie?" he said, squinting. But it was obvious. Cobb must have watched a lot of old films as well, because taking the holdall off his shoulder he started to walk forward saying, "Give me the gun, son." Albie thought back to Jack Gaughan's sweaty pleas on Nicky's bed. Albie suddenly realised what guns did to people. Guns turn people into bad actors, that's what they do.

"Inspector Cobb," said Albie, "I don't think you realise the importance of this case..."

Cobb was almost on top of him. He made a clumsy swipe at the gun and pulled it upwards but Albie's index finger was jerking at the trigger. One shot shattered the glass above the bathroom door. Albie closed his eyes. Cobb threw his large hands over his furry hat. A second shot ricochetted off the hall wall and Cobb dived for cover. Number three shot hit the fusebox on the wall. There was a spark and all the lights went out.

The only light now came from the outside lobby, which shone oblong-shaped through the open doorway. Three silhouettes moved into the oblong. One in a smart suit and the others with tall pointy heads.

The three people entered the hallway. The two pointy heads were uniformed PCs and the third was a small, plain-clothes dapper man. It was Commander Powell.

Albie felt tears well up in his eyes. Images of sewing mailbags in a five-by-five cell and rock breaking on some wind-blasted Dartmoor heath quick-marched through his mind. That it should all come to this.

Albie threw the pellet-gun down on the hallway floor. It scudded across the polished tiles. Albie sat on the floor with his head between his knees and started to cry. "Bugger it," he said. "I've had enough. Take me away, for Christ's sake. I've lost all of my mates, my job, and even my mum's going off abroad without telling me. Chuck me in a hole, eh? There's nothing left here."

The three figures stood in silence during Albie's outburst. After a polite pause they then turned to Cobb who, looking for cover, had submerged himself into the layers of coats and jackets hung up on hooks by the door.

"Detective Inspector Cobb," Commander Powell began, "I am placing you under arrest. You have the right to remain silent but I must warn you that anything you do say... and you know the rest of it yourself, Cobb."

Albie jerked his head up.

"Arrest *me*," said Cobb, his voice a whisper. "Arrest *me*?"

"That's right" said Commander Powell, sounding quite pleased with himself.

Cobb shook his head. "On what charge, for heaven's sake?"

"On account of you being the Hackney Bear."

Cobb moved his mouth but nothing came out.

"The holding charge will be the wasting of police time," said Commander Powell, "but I'm sure we'll find a few other things to chuck in as well."

"The Hackney Bear," said Cobb, his voice getting steadily louder. "I'm not the Hackney Bear. I'm the one who's been trying to find the Hackney Bear."

"You're finished, Cobb," said the dapper man.

"But why?" said Cobb, fighting to extricate himself from the confusion of coats.

The Commander began to laugh. "*Why*?" he spluttered.

"Come on, Cobb. You've been lucky to get away with it for as long as you have."

"Get away with what?" demanded Cobb.

"With being a loony." Powell turned to the two uniformed officers who were standing shoulder to shoulder in the doorway. "Take him away, fellas," he said, waving a hand dismissively.

Albie got to his feet. "Wait," he called. The officers stopped and turned towards him, as if they'd forgotten he was there.

"Listen," said Albie. "Listen. I can tell you something else about Cobb; something else that's dead important. It's to do with the Nicky Turner inquest."

"Albie," shouted Cobb, "what are you saying, son?"

Albie continued: "Cobb's brother-in-law was the copper who bust Nicky's head in but Cobb altered the log to make it look like he was never there. Don't you see? Cobb is covering up for a murder. If we can bring this to the inquest before it ends it'll mean the killer will be brought to trial. Don't you see?"

There was another pause before Commander Powell burst out laughing again. "Incredible. Unbelievable," he proclaimed. "If I understand your garbled story correctly, you're telling me that Detective Inspector Cobb here is an accomplice to murder after the fact. Ridiculous." The man moved a few feet towards Albie. There was almost a spring in his step.

"We've got as much as we need on Cobb," he said, "commandeering police vehicles for private use, abuse of authority, discreditable conduct, neglect of duty, falsehood, prevarication, consorting with known criminals, carrying out unauthorised investigations, claiming false expenses... you know, all the things that every copper does, day in day out."

Albie shook his head. "But the falsified documents," he

blurted out, "isn't that more important than all that lot put together?"

Commander Powell shrugged and stopped smiling. "Don't you think that bringing all that into the open might cause more problems than it would solve?" he asked wearily. "Think of others for a change, eh, Albie? I mean, it would affect the careers of countless other officers." The man softened his tone. "Listen, Albie, I'll be straight with you. I don't know how much you know but you've obviously been on the right track. I must admit I was surprised when you caught me keeping surveillance on Ronnie Riley and PC Currie at Hammersmith."

Cobb looked confused. He started to say something but Commander Powell cut across him. "Since you told me that Cobb here had been sticking his nose into this case unofficially, I discovered, as you may already know, that PC Rivers of the Special Patrol Group is his brother-in-law. I also discovered that Officers Rivers, Currie and Green have strong links with one of the extreme right-wing groups who pulled out of the November 5th march. I now have reason to believe that they only pulled out because those three officers conspired with them to cause an affray – making it look like the marchers were just a bunch of troublemakers and devaluing their cause."

Cobb looked horrified. "Believe me, Albie," he said. "I knew nothing about this, nothing at all."

Powell continued: "Cobb may well be telling the truth, Albie. You see, the confusion in Circle Square presented our three officers with a God-given opportunity. They didn't intend to actually kill anybody but once they did they immediately leaned on Cobb here, telling him it had all been a ghastly accident. He agreed out of loyalty to his brother-in-law."

Albie remembered his conversation in the Pie & Mash shop with Ginger. Of course, it was this deal which O was

157

now threatening to expose unless strings were pulled to fend off a Football Association enquiry into United. Think how it would look – Nicky had died because of an arrangement between the police and some fascists.

"But this should all be told to the inquest," cried Albie.

Powell smiled condescendingly. "I think we should be concerned with damage limitation at this stage, don't you? Be assured that the three officers in question will soon be eased out of the force on some pretext or other. Also, we'll be seen to be pulling in a corrupt DI. Cobb here. Your lefty chums will like that. The press will have something to write about and will forget all about Circle Square, and the public will be satisfied that we're capable of clearing up our own backyard. Everybody's happy! Why aren't you happy, Albie?"

"Because the bastard who killed my mate will go free, that's why."

Commander Powell moved forward again and put his arm gently on Albie's shoulder. "You can't bring back the dead, son."

Cobb started towards the man but the two PCs grabbed an arm apiece. "Listen," he shouted. "I know I took things into my own hands a bit but it's all turned out for the best, hasn't it? You said so yourself."

The man turned to face Cobb. "It may be that your maverick actions have saved a lot of embarrassment in the long run," he said, "but you still did wrong, Cobb. Not that it's in our interests to make that wrong known to the general public, of course."

"You know what this is, don't you?" said Albie.

"Yes," said Commander Powell. "It's a cover-up. A complete whitewash."

"Listen," pleaded Cobb, "you don't have to arrest me. I'll take early retirement from the Force. If I'm found guilty I could end up inside. You know as well as I do the sort of life a convicted copper has inside. A life like hell." Cobb was starting to lose control. He tried to struggle free of the uniformed officers and his furry hat slipped off, revealing for the first time his bald scalp. "I've got savings," shouted Cobb to Commander Powell. "I'll give you money to forget all about this. All three of you." He looked from side to side at the policemen. "For mercy's sake," he cried.

Commander Powell nodded to the PCs and they started to move Cobb out of the door.

Cob started to struggle violently and kick at the policemen who strong-armed him to the lift. "Help me, Albie," he called behind him, an arm outstretched, as they carried him off to toss him into the pit which he himself had dug. Commander Powell followed on.

They were gone. Albie stood shivering and open-mouthed. It wasn't the shock of seeing Cobb hauled away in such a fashion that had appalled him so much as those last words. *Help me, Albie*. Did Cobb really think he could? Or would? *Help me, Albie. Help me, Albie.* The words turned over and over in Albie's mind until they didn't sound like proper words any more, just a meaningless, unintelligible chant.

Albie had to work hard to cast off the spell. He moved through the dark hallway to the telephone and, straining his eyes, peered through the book for Pope's number. Even though tomorrow was the last day of the inquest, Commander Powell could be summoned and asked about Cobb's complicity.

As Albie put his hand on the receiver, it started to ring. It was Tommy with the one eye. "Listen, pal," he said, "you and me have been through a lot together. Remember when we were kids and you hauled me off the railway tracks just seconds before the Southend train came through? Remember how I slipped you a fiver a week regular for a year to help you and your mum when your dad died? Remember how we fought over that Maltese bird who worked in the Atlas Cafe but decided in the end she could go stuff herself, that it wasn't worth our friendship?'' There were tears in Tommy with the one eye's voice. ''Me and you, Albie, have always had a special understanding.''

Albie was very moved. He found it all the more moving because absolutely nothing Tommy with the one eye was saying was true.

Tommy with the one eye continued. ''My advice is to get out of that flat now, Albie. I don't know how long you've got. Go and stay somewhere else tonight, Albie. Can you hear me? Bad things are going to happen.''

Albie heard voices at the door, and felt a cold sweat break out on his forehead. Tommy with the one eye was still talking as Albie replaced the telephone receiver. One of the voices at the doorway was Rummy's and another was O's.

''Look, the door's wide open,'' Albie heard O say.

''And the lights aren't working,'' said Rummy, clicking the hallway light switch up and down. ''Electricity must be off.''

''Just as well we brought our own sounds,'' said a third voice. It was Ginger.

Albie moved slowly away from the telephone table and into the living room. When O, Rummy and Ginger entered, they found Albie in the centre of the room clutching a heavy, long stemmed vase in his fist.

''I'm not going to make it easy for you,'' he said, and started to swing the vase round and round his head like a medieval cudgel.

With another burst of adrenalin, the second that evening, pumping through his body, Albie began to feel

160

elated. At times he almost wanted to giggle. He felt no fear – and that frightened him.

The chubby figure of O stood in the centre of the group with his arms folded. "Come, come, Albie," he laughed, "what do you take us for, a bunch of yobboes?"

All three visitors were dressed in smart white overalls and heavy workmen's boots. "I mean," continued O, "it might be all right to fillet some young Paki down Brick Lane in the dead of night or push in the teeth of some Greenham Common lezzie now and then but we're not going to go round blacking the eye of a lad such as yourself with such important pals. How can we crack the ribs of a chap who gets his picture in the newspaper or bloody the nose of a man who gets his every word reported on the television?"

Albie let his arms drop but continued to swing the heavy vase around just inches from the carpet.

"Don't think I wouldn't like to give you a pasting, mind," said Rummy, barely able to contain himself. O unfolded his arms and signalled calm.

It was Ginger's turn next. "I feel the same, Albie," she said. "It's only loyalty to O that stops me parting your hair with a mallet."

"You good people didn't have to come here in person to tell me how much you liked me," said Albie. "You could have sent a postcard."

O laughed, rocking back on his heels.

When the threesome had first entered, it had looked to Albie as if Ginger was carrying a small suitcase. But now, as she placed the object at her feet, Albie could see that it was in fact a smart new ghettoblaster. From somewhere in the hallway Albie thought he could hear movement and he hoped that it was the police returning.

O smiled. He was obviously having a great time. "It's a pity we are – superficially at least – on opposite sides of the fence, Albie," he said. "You know, there's not a lot that divides us. We've both understood and developed a hatred of the current status quo, both have a desire to change the system, both have an awareness of the helplessness of the individual within the capitalist, foreign-financed market-place. It would have been so easy, Albie. If only you'd have spoken up for us at the inquest, told them that you and Nicky were patriots and that it was the reds' fault that Nicky's dead."

"That's right," snapped Ginger, "why wouldn't you ever say why you went on the march that day?"

"OK, OK," said Albie, not really sure where his mouth was taking him. "So you're all here to sing the praises of Nicky, are you? Well, I'll tell you something about that march and why Nicky died." The smile left O's face. "Perhaps Nicky was starting to see things a bit more clearly, perhaps he saw things a little differently to you lot. He went on that march plainly and simply because he believed in the cause and he was killed because of a plan hatched between some of the SPG officers and your pal O here…"

Ginger put her hands over her ears. "Shut up, shut up, you bastard," she shouted. Rummy bent down to press the ON button of the giant cassette player. At the sound of the jolly piano intro, O went to the door of the hallway, shoved a fat index finger between his lips and whistled. Almost immediately, the wide frame of Dirk, also wearing white overalls, entered the living room carrying a thick rubber bucket in each hand. Children's voices started to ring out of the ghettoblaster. It was the Ovaltinies:

> *Happy days are here again,*
> *the skies above are clear again,*
> *let us sing a song of cheer again…*

Albie let the heavy vase drop to the carpet. It landed with a neat *bomp* sound. Dirk placed the buckets on the floor and left the room. Rummy and Ginger picked up one each and a slop of white liquid splashed over the edge of Ginger's bucket, making a large seagull-shit shape on the carpet.

"Oi," said Albie.

> *...All together shout it now,*
> *there's no one who can doubt it now,*
> *so let's tell the world about it now,*
> *happy days are here again...*

O started to wave his arms about in time to the jaunty music in the manner of an old-time bandleader. He was bouncing up and down, quite light on his feet for a man of his proportions.

Dirk returned with more full buckets.

"All this could have been avoided by just a few well-chosen words from you, Albie," said O, conducting furiously.

"Words?" questioned Albie, raising his voice above the noise of the Ovaltinies.

> *...Your cares and troubles are gone,*
> *there'll be no cares from no on,*
> *happy days...*

"Words can start wars, Albie. Words can kill people. But they can stop people doing bad things as well. You didn't use the right words, Albie."

The buckets kept on coming until Albie asked, "You too, Dirk?"

"Don't take it personal, Albie," said Dirk, at pains to explain himself, "but I always told you I could only support you for as long as was convenient. And you can't ask for any more than that these days."

Albie nodded. "I guess you're right," he said.

And then Dirk lifted high one of the buckets and started to pirouette round and round, round and round in the centre of the room to the sounds of the Ovaltinies, the contents of the bucket splaying across all the walls.

The others joined in.

Chapter 22

Someone was ringing on the doorbell. It woke Albie up. He was lying flat down, fully clothed on top of the bedsheets. At first, he wondered who could be calling at this hour of the day but then he realised that he didn't know what hour of the day it was. In fact, it was only the light flooding into the room which told him it was day rather than night. Now, why hadn't he drawn the curtains the evening before? Albie's left arm was hanging off the side of the bed, the back of his hand flat on the floor. When he raised it to look at his watch he noticed that his palm was caked in white paint as was the face of the wristwatch. Somebody rang the doorbell again.

As Albie got up, the top bedsheet came with him, and pulling it away, he found that it had been glued to his front by great dollops of paint on his jeans and T-shirt.

Albie wandered slowly through all the rooms of the flat. Everywhere, huge circular splashes of paint decorated the walls, ceilings and floors. The Christmas tree had been scrunched into a corner under what looked like a surfeit of icing. All the pictures of Mum and Cobb's wedding had been whited out and a covering of paint made the TV set appear as if it had been carved out of stone. In fact, because of the white covering, almost every item – coffee tables, books and records – had taken the oddness of objects never before seen. Albie supposed he could open up the flat as a sort of avant-garde art gallery. All the while, somebody continued to ring the doorbell.

The hallway had been particularly disfigured. The backs of all the coats on the hangers were white and long stalactites of dried paint hung down from the ceiling, making the place look like some undiscovered subterranean cave.

Whoever was ringing the bell was very insistent. It flashed through Albie's mind that it might be O and his chums returning to do a second coat. But he supposed it didn't matter. There wasn't much more damage they could do. As he passed the mirror by the door, Albie could see that his face was speckled and that the paint in his hair made it stick up at wild punky angles.

A young man stood on the doorstep, a woman peering resentfully out from behind his shoulder. The man was angry but had obviously scripted his piece.

"'Scuse me pal," he said, "I'm not one to make complaints like, far from it – live and let live is my motto – but the noise coming from your flat last night was a bit over the top. Downstairs it sounded like you were all jumping up and down like a bunch of loonies. Now, we like a party ourselves but we've got an eleven-month-old nipper, you see, and it woke her right up..."

As the man carried on talking, Albie noticed that the scowl of the woman's face turned to curiosity as she gazed past Albie down the whitewashed hallway. She nudged her husband's side.

The man was coming to the end of his tirade. "...I don't object to parties, pal," he reiterated, "all I ask is a little consideration for others, that's all. The kid and that. You see what I mean, pal?"

Albie nodded slowly. "Yeah, sorry 'bout that," he said stupidly. "I had a few friends round who, er, like to paint the town a bit."

Having said his piece, the man at the door focused on Albie's clothes for the first time. He moved his eyes up and down the paint-stained jeans and T-shirt and slowly took in the background.

"Well, just so long as we know where we stand," he said without his former confidence. There was an embarrassing pause before the woman started to tug at the man's shirt. "Well, we'll let you get back to your decorating," he said, backing away. "No hard feelings, eh?"

Albie was still in a haze. He laughed inappropriately. "No," he called out as they scurried back downstairs. "No hard feelings at all."

Albie closed the door and went into the bathroom. He turned the shower on, thinking that he might be able to wash the shock of the previous night's visit down the plughole. He undressed slowly, a dreaming man. He let the shower run cold, not caring a bit. Very slowly the emulsion became unclogged from his hair. It slid smoothly down over his face. He had to push it out of his eyes. He stood with his mouth open, and catching sight of himself in the bathroom mirror he thought he looked like pictures he'd seen of South American hunters who covered their entire bodies with thick, chalky paste. And he felt at that moment that he too was a hunter stalking prey in a rainforest at the edge of the world.

The telephone rang as Albie was drying himself. It was Mum, frantic. She'd waited all night and all day at the airport and Cobb hadn't turned up. Yeah, well, it's like this, Albie told her. He'd had a bit of a row with Cobb and tried to shoot him but the coppers had come and arrested him saying he was the Hackney Bear and later on some fascists had dropped in to wreck the place. Albie heard Mum start to cry. This was serious, she said. This was no time to be funny. Her words stopped Albie dead. He realised the ridiculousness of what he was saying. Sorry, Mum, he told her. Cobb had been called away on an urgent case. He had left a message that Mum was to fly out on the very next flight. Cobb would follow on ASAP. Mum calmed down a bit but said she wasn't sure about that at all. But it's all booked up, isn't it? said Albie, the hotel and everything? Well, then, why don't you go then? Mum said she'd never flown before. Albie said that it was about time she did. And Cobb had said to say that he loved her. 'Bye, Mum.

Now that the paint had been washed away from the face of his watch Albie could see that it was already early evening. Looking at the dark settling on the East End rooftops, Albie realised with horror that he must have slept for the whole of the inquest's last day. He dressed in a hurry and retrieved the pellet-gun from under the telephone table where it had scraped to a halt the night before. He scrubbed it with a hard brush and Ajax under the bathroom tap and, picking it up with a pencil rammed in the barrel slid it into a plastic bag. He shoved it down the rubbish chute on his way out.

Tina wasn't in when he called at her place so he decided to go to the Popes' in case she was there. He bought an evening newspaper on the way. The headline said: SPG ABSOLVED BY CIRCLE SQUARE JURY.

Isabella Pope opened the door in answer to Albie's urgent rapping. She said not a word but spun on her heels and led Albie through the screen of giant rubber plants into the spacious studio flat. At first, Albie thought that she must be angry with him for some reason, but she gusted silently through the room, where Simon Pope and Detective Sergeant Starling were sitting. Albie realised that it was Hubby she had it in for.

Pope and Detective Sergeant Starling sat on large sagbags while Pope's two boys played round them. Starling didn't look comfortable at all. He was still wearing a coat and sitting bolt upright – which isn't easy on a sagbag.

"Didn't see you in the Coroner's Court for the inquest verdict," drawled Pope in a lazy yet accusatory tone.

"Yeah, well, I went to a party instead, you see? It was called at short notice in my flat and I only got a last-minute invitation. What's all this stuff in the paper about the police being absolved?" Albie waved the tabloid in the air.

Pope sighed. "The jury returned a verdict of misadventure rather than unlawful killing on the coroner's direction. Parkinson-Kettle's summing up was totally biased in favour of the police. He branded all witnesses as unreliable, even those with head injuries, and then had the cheek to insinuate that if the police had hit Turner it was only with reasonable force and with no intention to seriously injure or kill – hence misadventure. The coppers in the court looked delighted. The INCIDENT members in the gallery started to boo and the place was cleared."

A cello started to play somewhere. But unlike the slow sad hum it made on Albie's first visit here it was now making angry, spiky cuts in the air.

"The whole thing's crazy," said Starling. "The fact that the police aren't even investigating the death is a virtual admission that they think an officer was responsible. With this verdict they'll say there was no murder, no manslaughter, to look into."

"And what about you?" Albie asked Starling.

The policeman shrugged. "I've thought about resignation, of course," he said, head down, "but I'll stay on. I can only justify it by telling myself that I'll be keeping the others under permanent surveillance. And why should I quit?" He lifted his head. "I'd hate to see the day when all the honest coppers felt obliged to go off and become supermarket security men."

"What's all this about a demo?" demanded Albie,

unfolding the newspaper in front of Pope.

Pope shook his head. "It's a whole lot of nonsense, Albie. Ignore it. Ironically, since Denny's death, Tina has been obsessed more than ever with Turner's death."

Albie said: "It says in this article that outside the court after the verdict Tina told reporters that she was planning some sort of Christmas Eve protest march against the decision. She reckons she can raise over three hundred INCIDENT members for tonight."

"A purely emotional gesture," said Pope.

The scratchy cello onslaught ceased. Isabella's voice rang out from the other room. "Heaven forbid that any-body should get emotional about such a small thing as murder."

Pope smiled in what he no doubt hoped was a com-radely fashion to the gathering of men. "Don't shout, darling," he called, "you'll wake the girls."

Starling shifted awkwardly on the sagbag, obviously embarrassed at being present at a marital row. It occurred to Albie that he'd never seen Starling comfortable in *any* situation he'd seen him in.

"The plain truth, Albie," said Pope, lowering his voice, "is that since the Public Order Bill was passed, six days' notice will have to be given before the march can take place and one person named as organiser. Also they'll have to arrange a route with the police. Tina hasn't done any of this in which case she could be liable to three months' prison or a whacking great fine. Even just being a partici-pant on such a march could mean big trouble."

Isabella appeared at the doorway, leaning up against the frame. "Well, we wouldn't want to go breaking the law now, would we?" she said sarcastically.

"Darling, it may have slipped your mind that I am putting myself forward for selection as a parliamentary candidate in the New Year. If I end up in court, I can kiss all that goodbye."

"Bloody parliamentary candidate."

"Darling! In the long run, the advances I could make for similar causes to INCIDENT from an influential position will far outweigh any conceivable value in taking part in this stupid adventure."

"Simon, at this time more than any other Tina needs our support," said Isabella.

"Darling, the best way we can support Tina on this issue is by not supporting her."

Isabella laughed and stomped off back to the other room. Starling looked more embarrassed than ever.

"Where does the march start?" asked Albie. "I must see Tina as soon as possible."

"Albie," said Pope thoughtfully, holding his hands palm to palm at his chin, "I really don't think it would be in your best interests to tell you. Not that I believe in pointlessly withholding information, of course."

"Jago Gardens in Shoreditch," called Isabella from the other room.

Pope sniffed. "Thank you *very* much, darling," he said.

Chapter 23

Albie started to run as soon as he left the Popes' flat. He was out of breath even before he reached the Highway. He couldn't think of any buses that went directly to Shoreditch. Besides, checking the change in his pocket, he found that he only had twenty-seven pence on him. Not enough for a bus fare. So he hailed a cab instead.

Albie just yelled "Shoreditch" at the slightly startled cabbie and jumped in the back. The cabbie pulled open the glass partition and tilted his head in Albie's direction. "Whereabouts in Shoreditch?" he asked. Albie told him he'd let him know when they got nearer and the cab pulled away.

They sped through the East London backstreets, past the brightly-lit pubs, people jostling elbow to elbow at the bar, past the Laughing Plaice fish & chip shop packed with hungry customers, past the flats and houses where couples cuddled up in front of the Christmas telly, past the larking teenagers on the littered youth-club steps. Albie had never felt so alone.

"Bit of a rum verdict in that Circle Square inquest, wasn't it, mate?" the cabbie shouted backwards to Albie.

"Was it?" said Albie. "I haven't been following the case much myself."

It was a short ride, not quite a quarter of an hour. They were a few blocks away from Jago Gardens when Albie spotted a slim alleyway with a row of Victorian bollards across it to stop vehicles attempting to drive down it. "You can stop here, driver," called Albie. The meter had clocked up way over what Albie possessed. Albie got out and poked his head into the front of the cab. "I want you to know, driver, that I've never bilked a cabbie in the past and I never will again. It's not in my nature. It undermines the unity of labour, you see? But tonight, well, you just struck unlucky."

And tossing the twenty-seven pence he had into the cab Albie sped away on his toes down the alleyway before the cabbie could even raise his voice. Albie ran blindly, not sure of the exact location of Jago Gardens, but glimpsing a glow in the sky beyond the rooftops and sniffing smoke drifting along from that direction he had a feeling that that was the way he should be heading.

Turning a corner, Albie could see a mass of people on the littered oval which went by the name of Jago Gardens. Several tower blocks overlooked the gardens and Albie could make out the shapes of the inhabitants at their windows looking out to see what was going on below.

The glow in the sky which had led Albie here was coming from a huge bonfire in the centre of the gardens, round which the marchers were gathering. Bright, burning cinders floated out of the crackling flames and away into the dark night sky. They seemed to roll in the air in formation before blackening and vanishing in the cold.

Some of the gathering stood stamping their cold feet into the patchy grass and warming their hands by the flames, palms outward. Some had banners, as yet unfurled. Voices were high and strangely cheery in an expectant rush of urgency. An old woman, a lit sparkler in each woolly gloved hand, was dancing in the smoke round the perimeter of the bonfire. Albie circled the flames, looking for Tina.

There seemed to be an endless variety of people in Jago Gardens, ranging from pudgy middle-aged men with thick curly beards to lean young punks with multicoloured hair. Albie recognised some of the people from the INCIDENT meetings he'd been to with Denny. He had never realised how many people were now involved in the campaign.

Albie stopped running round the bonfire and caught hold of the sleeve of a woman with plaited hair and a young baby in a pouch on her breast. "Tina, have you seen Tina?" he shouted. "Who?" she asked. He asked an old man in a duffel coat and round, owlish spectacles. A child was playing at his feet. The old man turned his back on Albie as the little boy released his grip on the strings of a bunch of black balloons he was holding. They pop-pop-popped in the heat of the fire. Albie approached a young couple with scarves tied round their mouths like bandits. "And who are you?" the man demanded. "Special Branch?"

At last, Albie saw Tina's beaten-up old car parked under an area shadowed by trees.

Albie started to run across. The car boot was open and Albie could see some people pulling garments out from a large wicker basket inside it. Some of the figures were already costumed from head to foot in long hoods and gowns. One of the figures turned as Albie approached. The person's face was a skull. Albie stopped dead, catching his breath.

Slowly, a slim, dark gloved hand moved out of the folds of the gown to remove the mask. It was Tina.

"Tina," said Albie, "I just had to come and talk to you. I've got a confession to make." Tina's face was as immobile as the mask she had just removed. "The truth is," he told her, "that I never went on that demonstration with Nicky. Not one bit of it. Nicky told me that he was going on it and I went as far as Oxford Street with him before we split up. But when all the fuss started and people assumed I'd been with him I just let them believe it. It made me feel important."

Albie was still out of breath from running. He ran his

fingers through his sweaty hair. "That march was the biggest thing that ever happened to me in my life, Tina, and I never even went on it."

Tina smiled. "Well," she said, "you're on it now."

Tina stood on one of Jago Gardens' little wooden benches to address the crowd. With the cowl of her cape round her neck and the flames behind her, Albie thought she looked like a witch about to be burned at the stake.

The crowd were silent as she started to speak. She told them firmly that they were to follow the front marchers closely, as they alone knew the exact route the march was to take. They were heading for Circle Square where they would maintain a torchlight vigil throughout the night. They weren't just marching for Nicky Turner who had been so obviously murdered but for those whom the state had killed in other ways – old people from hypothermia, women through murder and rape, men from stress and workers through accidents at work. "I'm warning you all now that under new laws just passed by parliament this gathering is illegal. It is taking place without the permission of the state. But a right to protest at the discretion of those you are protesting against is no right at all. The streets belong to the people – and we won't be forced off them! Can they legislate against fury?"

"No," the marchers chorused. Leaping from the bench to light her torch at the bonfire flames, Tina led them all out of Jago Gardens. The front marchers, about a dozen or so, all pulled their skull masks up across their faces and their hoods over their heads. Those marchers who had a torch filed past the bonfire one by one, dipping them into the flames. One of the onlookers from the surrounding tower blocks shouted out something from between cupped hands. It sounded something like, "they're gonna screw you".

Albie, despite his lack of costume, marched at the front with Tina. Tina explained that the heads of the torches had been doused in paraffin so that they wouldn't easily be put out by the light snow which was just starting to flutter down from the black sky.

It was a very cold night and Albie wasn't really dressed for it. He pulled the collar of his raincoat up tight. The march was properly on its way now, a long fiery snake of people and placards winding its way along the night-time London streets.

Despite it being almost midnight, there were quite a few people about. Heads poked out of the festively decorated pubs as the marchers moved through Old Street. A couple of beery men, pint glasses in hand and with silly Christmas hats on their heads, stared out in disbelief at the skeletal front marchers tramping through the Shoreditch streets. Tina told Albie that the masks and costumes, which they'd borrowed from a sympathetic theatre group, were as much for protection as effect. As organisers they could be heavily fined – "If they find out who we are," said Tina speaking with difficulty through the hideous rubber creation.

They soon moved into the business centre of the city where there were few places open and the streets were empty. Albie told Tina about the day Nicky died. "He said he was going on some demo or other," he explained. "I didn't really know much about it at the time. I wasn't even very interested."

"So you didn't know why he was going?"

"I didn't know why *anybody* went on marches. But now I know why people protest so I guess that means I know why Nicky went as well."

Tina nodded.

"To be honest, Tina, for a long time I didn't really know

176

whether he'd been on the march or whether he was just looking for trouble like people have been saying. But now I know."

"What made up your mind?"

"I just feel certain that if Nicky was alive today he'd be on this march with us tonight."

There was a pause before Tina burst out laughing. "If Nicky Turner was alive *we* wouldn't be on this march," she said.

"Yeah, I suppose so," said Albie. "Just imagine that, we wouldn't be here."

Just ahead of them in the wide Cheapside street were two beat bobbies walking in their direction. Their conversation with each other was curtailed as they looked towards each other and then back at the marchers. Both bobbies looked quite young, only months older than Albie, perhaps. As the marchers approached, torches burning, skull-faced demons to the fore, they obviously had no idea what they should do. They began to speak with urgency into their radios.

"Fire with fire," said Tina. She pulled the mask away from her face and looking furtively about her reached inside the folds of her black gown. Albie didn't know what Tina meant until she produced what he took at first to be a tacky children's toy, a bright red thing with plastic knobs and buttons. Tina spoke into it. It was a CB radio. "I figured we'd need all the help from above that we could muster," she said, and whispering something into the handset, she passed it across to Albie.

"Hi there, Albie," said a scratchy voice.

Tina explained that it was a transceiver, a combination of transmitter and receiver. "You press this thing here when you want to speak into it," instructed Tina. Albie pressed this thing here and said "Who is it?"

"Don't you recognise my voice, Albie?"

"Donald bloody Duck," said Albie.

"It's Elliott, Elliott Ness. Me and Tina worked out beforehand that along the route of the march there's a whole series of tower blocks and tall buildings from where I can keep an aerial view of you all. Think of me as your guardian angel. I'm here to let you know of any approaching oppo. In fact," said Ness, a note of concern creeping into his tone, "I can see a police car on its way to you right now. Looks like they're intending to cut you off at Holborn Viaduct. I need to get to the next vantage point now but I'll be back in touch soon."

Almost at once, a police car, its siren uncharacteristically silent, screeched to a halt in the middle of the street directly in front of the marchers. The driver and two other uniformed officers, one of them chewing gum, stepped sharply out, the driver confidently flipping open a notepad and licking the tip of his pencil.

Tina turned to the body of silent marchers. "Just keep going," she yelled, waving her torch above her head, before pulling the death's-head mask back over her face.

To their credit, the policemen looked only mildly horrified as the marchers parted and flooded around them on both sides, as wilfully oblivious to them and their car as a cattle stampede to a pony and trap.

The gum-chewing policeman immediately reached into the back of the vehicle and produced a loud hailer. He clicked it on, and, spitting out the gum, bellowed into the tail of the march. "Listen, you lot. I'm giving you fair warning. It is an arrestable offence to take part in a banned demonstration – which I have to inform you is the case with this one since it was brought to the attention of the Home Secretary earlier today..."

The marchers, who all the time had maintained a deathly silence, now on Tina's instruction, began to whoop-whoop-whoop in the manner of Red Indians in the films, palms fiercely flapping against opened mouths. It had the effect of drowning out the loud-hailer drone entirely.

Albie and Tina started to talk about the inquest verdict while the other marchers continued to whoop-whoop-whoop it up. "I can't say that I'm surprised at the result," said Tina.

Albie nodded. "Sounds like it'll be a vindication of the SPG rather than an indictment. Because it's been dragged all through the court they've been *proved* to be blameless."

"I must admit, though," said Tina, "that I wouldn't be satisfied if PC Rivers or any individual policeman were sent to trial. The Force wins either way. If a copper gets convicted he serves as a scapegoat and if he gets acquitted the police are exonerated. The whole bloody show stays on the road. Nicky's death was a state crime, Albie. It's a terrible thing to say – but if the coppers are given the job of keeping the lid on such a rotten system some people are bound to get burned. They're not employed as social workers, you know."

Over the CB radio, the crackly voice of Elliott Ness could be heard. He told Tina that another two police cars were approaching along High Holborn to try and cut them off. He informed them that if they skipped through Brook Way, a small alleyway too slim for cars, the police wouldn't be able to follow. So that's what they did.

The snow was coming down steadily now and Albie soon felt very wet. Tina's costume was heavy with it and was no longer black but speckled white. The marchers' flaming torches crackled and fizzed in the downfall, some being extinguished altogether.

They trudged on, Tina and Albie chattering at one another at a fast pace. Most of the marchers had lapsed once more into silence, worried at the escalating police

179

presence. Albie felt nervous. He said: "I only realised today that all this time I've been expecting Nicky to return, especially once the inquest was over. I've been thinking – OK, Nicky, you've made your point but you can come out now, all the fuss has died down. I think I felt the same when my dad died, that once all the formalities of the funeral were over he could come back home again."

"Whenever I think about Denny," said Tina, "I think, well, what's occupying the space he took up while he was alive? Does it leave us with a Denny-sized piece of surplus air to breathe?"

Elliott Ness announced that he'd have to move to another building again. He couldn't see anything on the horizon at the moment – back soon. What happened next, however, didn't need an aerial view, for all eyes were soon scanning the skies to see where the swishing sounds were coming from. Suddenly, from over the rooftops a low-flying helicopter swept into view, a circling beam from its belly soon locating and spotlighting the front of the march.

Because of the harsh light, Albie found it hard to see ahead of him. Tina had tucked the CB radio away again and Albie automatically held on to her free hand. She responded by squeezing it tight. The buzz of the helicopter increased as the machine hovered just above them, the beating blades cutting through the snow-choked air. The roaring bird slid sharply from left to right over the marchers, the giant torchlight all the time remaining fixed on them.

The downfall of snow increased greatly in its intensity, extinguishing all the marchers' torches. Tina's still glowed a bit.

Despite the cold and the growing sense of danger, a feeling of impossible elation flooded Albie's mind. It was as if the march were a place to live, self-sufficient and complete, a strange new city he'd woken up in where he knew all the streets and houses. He felt excited in the way he'd get in the old days playing in Nicky's bedroom, as if a million years lay before them, an anticipation of future glory. And all at once Albie realised the terrible truth of Tina's simple observation that if Nicky were still alive they wouldn't even be there, that if it wasn't for the sacrifice of his friend, this awakening might never have happened. It was the ghost of Nicky who had beckoned Albie along the broad highways, led him through the winding alleyways and round the tricky turnings of this new town.

Up ahead, at the top of the street there was – and it was difficult to tell because of the thick snow and the light from the hovering craft – a wall of some sort, a solid dark wall about six feet high. The marchers automatically started to slow down; those with banners and placards letting them drop in an apologetic manner.

Shielding his eyes from the relentless beam, Albie looked directly ahead. Before them stood a human barricade of riot police. The line of fifty or so officers were dressed identically in heavy-duty overalls with a belt at the waist, and boots, gloves and shiny steel helmets with perspex visors. In one hand they carried a long thick baton and in the other a man-length see-through riot shield.

Albie felt the pressure on his hand increase. "There'll be fireworks now," said Tina.

Elliott Ness came back on the air.

"Holy Moses" he said. "It looks like you've come up against one hell of a roadblock."

Tina instructed all the marchers to stand still. She told Albie that no general ever leads an army into defeat no matter what the cause was. But she wasn't sure what to do now.

Elliott Ness provided the answer. "It's as clear as day,"

said the crackly voice through the transceiver. "If you take a detour down the street to your right and then left into Approach Street you'll find yourself facing a building site. There's a couple of panels from the surrounding corrugated iron missing. All you need to do is lead the marchers in and across the site to the other side. Just pull off another few panels of the fencing when you get there and you're standing right in Circle Square itself. The coppers won't believe it." Ness laughed at the brilliance of his plan.

Tina pulled the mask up off her face to the top of her head. She licked her lips thoughtfully. The whine of the helicopter engine above was making it difficult for Tina to communicate with the rest of the marchers. The plan was passed down the line by word of mouth. No sooner was the chain of information started however when there came a further loud-hailer warning. The officer's amplified voice warned that the marchers would have to disperse. He promised that no charges would be brought if they were willing to cooperate at this stage.

Nobody moved.

The timing for the operation depended on a hand signal from Tina. She couldn't really have been sure that her command had filtered along right to the back of the crowd. As it was, when she leapt up into the air, punching her black-gloved fist at the white speckled sky, all hell broke loose. The line of policemen must have mistaken it as a sign to launch an assault on them and started to move forward. At the same time, at the back of the march the uninformed demonstrators took the signal as a warning to flee the marauding police.

As the police squad approached the front of the crowd the marchers headed sharp right according to plan while the back of the march sped off in inglorious retreat. Children on the march began to cry out and shouts of confusion from the adults were made unintelligible by all the noise. Overhead, the helicopter came in low, its sweeping blades causing the hair on Albie's head to whip about furiously like grass on a windy hill.

As Elliott Ness had told them, the corrugated iron fence was just round the next corner. It blocked off the end of Approach Street, or would have done had it not been for the gaps. The front runners, who included Albie and Tina, were soon pouring through a hole.

"The police are right behind you," warned Elliott Ness, "and that big bloody bee is still buzzing overhead." This didn't need pointing out. The helicopter beat over them, its cruel beam spotlighting the marchers who were running across the site.

"They've picked off a few of the marchers at the back and are chucking them into vans," Elliott told them. "And they're dispersing pretty roughly the ones who ran the other way."

The huge square site within the corrugated iron walls was completely flat for the most part. The previous structure had only just been demolished, and they hadn't even started to dig foundations for the new one. Beneath the running marchers' feet was a pale, pasty goo, a combination of brick dust, chalky earth and snow turned to slush.

"Run like hell," shouted Tina, although nobody could have heard her out-of-breath voice as the helicopter scudded low over their heads. She threw off the mask perched on her head and untied the cords of the black cape around her neck so that it fluttered away behind her. The other costumed marchers did the same and the impression was of the sudden release of a dozen giant bats.

The machine above was coming in fast, churning the mud beneath their feet into sharp, treacly peaks. With her cape gone, Tina didn't have a large enough pocket for the

CB radio. She held it awkwardly in her hand as she ran. Albie was right beside her, his chest heaving.

"I'll take it," he panted.

"You'd better not," Tina said, between breaths, "they'll take you for one of the organisers if we get caught." He took it anyway.

There was a crackly voice coming out of the small box. "Jesus Christ," yelled a frantic Elliott Ness, "I don't believe it. They're gonna screw you, man, they're gonna screw you."

Albie pressed the button on the CB radio. "What's the matter, Elliott?" he asked. They were already halfway across the site. Up ahead, somebody was bashing out the teeth of corrugated iron from the outside all the way along. "They've got a whole damn mob of mounted police arriving," Elliott told him.

Even as Elliott spoke, Albie could see for himself the police breaking through. The officers on foot tossed the iron sheets inwards and there was a loud drumroll of hooves as the horses thudded in over them with baton-wielding policemen on their backs. They were dressed the same as the steel-helmeted police on foot but minus shields.

"They're gonna screw you, they're gonna screw you," came the chant over the radio but the beating of the horses' hooves and the noise of the heavy machine which bore down on them soon drowned everything else out. Albie couldn't even hear what Tina was shouting into his ear.

As the mounted army approached, Tina and Albie and the rest of the front runners halted, causing some of those behind to stagger and fall, slipping and sliding on the muddy surface of the site. The marchers automatically started to retreat, but on seeing the foot police who had pursued them through the fence, they fanned out into a wide, frightened circle, looking for exits, their feet plunging deep into the sticky paste.

A bizarre display of mud-wrestling ensued as police tried to grab hold of the demonstrators. The riot shields they carried proved an encumbrance as their heavy black boots slipped in the mud. Many tossed the shields aside while one fell on top of his and simply slid away, looking like some strange alien mud-surfer. Those police who tried to swipe at the marchers with their long sticks lost their balance and ended up face down in the goo while those who grabbed people bodily were soon cavorting on the ground with their prey in a disgusting, pasty embrace. People were starting to panic. They screamed, their open mouths big black holes in pale white faces.

Suddenly, and with a loud hiss of electricity, the whole site was bathed in a bright clear light as a huge arc light high above them was slammed on. The illumination must have been installed so that the builders could toil late into the dark winter afternoons. Albie caught sight of Tina, glimpsed through the net curtain of snowfall. They had become separated in the panic and she was over on the other side of the site, her bleached-out features twisted in a grimace. Albie only now noticed that he, like Tina, was coated from head to toe in the sticky, pale paste of the site.

The helicopter above them must have been hovering very low, for instead of throwing light down on top of them it covered them with threatening black shadows, blotting out whole groups of fleeing demonstrators as it obscured the arc light, its circling blades causing the mud to twist up and into the faces of marchers and police alike.

The police on horseback continued to pour through the wide gaps in the fence and ride across the site, causing people to run in all directions. Those marchers who still clutched screaming children cried for it all to stop. The horses seemed to have no trouble at all in moving across the mucky surface. They moved through gaggles of marchers, making them split up into smaller and smaller groups. Albie saw the old man in the owlish spectacles he'd spoken to earlier hit across the forehead by a casual blow from a police truncheon. He lay on the ground with his white-haired head in his hands. Over and over he rolled in the chalky paste.

The police on foot had obviously pulled themselves together and although, like everybody else, their clothes and skin were caked in the pale muck, they began to run along the inside of the corrugated perimeter, trailing their long sticks along the rutted sheet metal as they went, producing a threatening rat-tat-tat machine-gun thunder.

The noise from the helicopter engine rang even louder in Albie's ears as the spiteful thrashing machine came in fast. It seemed that the police were now on all four sides of the site. Some demonstrators were trying to climb out over the top while others battled pointlessly with the uniformed officers. And dead in the middle Albie circled round and round. He had lost sight of Tina altogether.

Suddenly, somebody was on him. A hand grabbed his shoulder tightly. Albie turned to gaze at his assailant, a shadowy figure glimpsed through the mud in his own eyes, a paste-caked figure almost unrecognisable as a man. Albie realised that in his attacker's eyes he was probably no longer a human being either. He thought of the image in the bathroom mirror – a hunter stalking prey in a rainforest at the edge of the world.

Albie clenched the CB radio tight in his fist and raised his hand automatically to defend himself. As he did so he accidentally caught the tall figure in the face. There was a red tinge on the small whitewashed transceiver. ''That's done it,'' thought Albie, realising that the man would think he was being attacked.

The figure raised one arm in protection and used the other to twist Albie's arm behind his back. Albie was pushed forward on to his knees and then face down into the pasty surface of the site. All round Albie was noise. With his head in the mud, the roar of the rotor blades, the throbbing engine and the screams of the protestors melded together in a long, loud plug-hole gurgle.

Albie felt the cold sticky mud all round his body as if it were embracing him, urging him to come-under-come-under. It filled his nostrils and ears and he shut his eyes automatically as it filled all the pores of his face. Just then, somewhere above the underwater thunder, Albie thought he could hear a voice – a woman's voice. Tina? Albie tried to call out to her but the icy mud slushed through the gaps in his teeth. It started to fill the cave of his mouth. There was pressure on the small of his back as though a giant boot were forcing him down, down deep with the dead of centuries.

Albie felt faint, very faint, and as the police helicopter circled overhead he imagined Cobb was standing above him, shining his torch round and round a big black hole.

"All the way to hell, Albie" said Cobb.

The boot got heavier and Albie couldn't breathe any more. He felt himself sinking down, sinking down.

Chapter 24

Albie and Nicky were in the park, standing once again by the boatless, shimmering lake. Nicky raised a finger to point out the figure approaching from the centre of a wide green plain, a light mist behind him.

The figure was Denny, of course. He smiled at them both, a wide, friendly smile. "Well," said Denny to Albie as he reached them, "aren't you going to introduce us?"

Albie was taken aback. "Of course!" he said, smacking his forehead with the palm of his hand. "You two have never met before, have you? Seems hard to believe. Denny, this is Nicky. Nicky, Denny." They shook hands.

"Heard a lot about you, Nicky," said Denny.

"Nice to meet you, Denny," said Nicky. "Thanks for all you've done. We're going to have to be off soon, you know?"

"But where are we going?" asked Albie.

Denny looked embarrassed. He told Albie: "I'm afraid you won't be coming with us. When Nicky said we had to be off he meant just him and me."

Nicky turned to Albie. "Well, this is it, I'm afraid, pal," he said, "we won't be meeting you again."

"You're kidding, not even now and then?"

Nicky shook his head. "Off to another place," he said.

"What's it like?" asked Albie.

"Where?"

"You know where I mean" said Albie.

It was Denny who answered. "It's a city of mirrors, Albie. Everything, absolutely everything and everybody are made of mirrors."

"What, postboxes, pavements and people's skins? All mirrors?"

"Everything, Albie. Even people's eyes are mirrors. So that everything and everybody are a reflection of everything and everybody else."

Albie drifted in and out of sleep. He could feel that he was lying on something soft. He felt nice and warm. He didn't care where he was or who the provider of this welcome comfort was. He was so tired. He couldn't even lift the lids of his eyes. It felt nice. He could only recall the vaguest of details of the time before this. Was it a day ago? A lifetime ago? He remembered the crush, the fight, the mud which filled his nostrils. He could only just bring back a memory of being hauled up from the sticky ground and being carried away on the arms of others. He thought he could remember being stood under a hot shower and perhaps he could remember being laid out on a sofa and a blanket being thrown over him.

He opened his eyes.

Albie was lying on the sofa in Denny and Tina's flat, the sofa on which he had slept so many nights in the past few months. Tina and Elliott Ness sat watching him. Ness sat at Denny's writing desk.

Albie sat up abruptly, his hand automatically running over the green jumper he was wearing. The jumper wasn't his, yet it was somehow familiar. It was the same with the dark trousers he had on.

"Your own clothes are soaking in the bath," Tina told him. "It was so cold that we thought you needed something on, though. They're Denny's old clothes."

Albie nodded.

"You've slept all through Christmas," said Tina. "You looked in a really bad state, but we decided against taking you to hospital. You'd have been arrested for sure. All the demonstrators who were left in that building site were nicked.''

"You mean that some got out?"

"We got out," said Ness. "From where I was watching from above I could see a space in the corrugated iron the police didn't have covered. I tried to tell you over the CB radio but nobody could hear by then. Everybody was running round like headless chickens.''

"How did we escape then?" Albie asked.

Ness grinned. "I got fed up with being an outside observer so I thought I'd come and get stuck in.''

"Elliott came to lead us out through the gap," said Tina. "He especially went looking for you. When he caught up with you, though, you belted him with the radio.''

"You mean it was Elliott who I...?"

Elliott smiled. He had a tooth missing.

Albie rubbed his head in his hands. Elliott went to make some tea. There was something different about Elliott. Albie realised it was that he didn't have his woolly Rasta hat on. His locks were much shorter than Albie had expected.

"It would be nice to see you again, Tina," said Albie after a while. "I've missed talking to you. I know what happened has changed things between us but we've sorted that out now, haven't we? Sort of.''

"Sure," said Tina, "we sorted things out.''

"What are you doing tonight?"

"I'm busy tonight," she told him. "I'm sort of seeing somebody. Know what I mean?''

Elliott came back with the teas.

"We need to do something for Denny," said Albie. "I've been thinking; it might be nice if we put together a little book of his poetry and got it published.''

Tina smiled. "Yeah, that's a great idea.''

Albie drank the tea down in one gulp and said he'd have to be going. Elliott said Albie should stay longer. He needed to recover properly. Albie said he'd be all right.

"So we'll meet up one of these days to select some of Denny's pieces, eh?" said Albie to Tina as he was putting on one of Denny's coats. Tina said that was a great idea too.

Albie said goodbye to Tina. She didn't approach him for a goodbye hug and a kiss as she would have done in the past, even on the most ordinary occasions. She just said goodbye.

Elliott went with Albie down the stairs. "I could always stay a little longer, of course," said Albie. "Will you be going back my way?"

Elliott grinned shyly. "No, mate," he said. "I'm staying here, sort of. You see?"

"I see," said Albie.

Albie is back home now.

Nobody has been to the flat high in the sky since the whitewash attack so nobody's tidied up. The place is a mess.

But first things first. A nice cup of tea and a look at the papers. The riot gets a garbled mention in some of them and wasn't serious enough for the others to mention. Nobody died this time.

The *Daily Informer* runs a story about a rumoured FA investigation into allegations of fascist infiltration at United's grounds. It seems that someone has sent them a newly-printed right wing leaflet with what was said to be club chairman Ronnie Riley's fat thumbprint on it. Did Ronnie Riley have anything to say? He says, depending on how things come out, he may have a lot to say indeed. The exclusive story is written by Jack Gaughan, now billed as the *Informer*'s "crusading journalist".

Albie smiles.

Albie drinks his tea and lies down on the sofa looking out of the window just above his head. He watches the upside down clouds roll past.

There are upside down birds too.

It is quiet in the flat, very quiet. It is quieter than Albie can remember it since Nicky died. He starts to think about food. It's been a long time since he's eaten and he's hungry. He figures that he can't put anything in the microwave because the electricity has been blown. So he thinks about going down to the Laughing Plaice fish & chip shop instead.

His body aches. He doesn't want to move.

The telephone starts to ring, shattering the dreamy silence. Albie doesn't know if he's been dozing or not. Sleeping and waking and dreaming. That's what life's all about, life is.

The telephone is bleeping but he can't get up. It could be anybody calling. It puts him in the frame of mind that he might do some phoning round himself.

Maybe he'll give Tommy with the one eye a call later on.